"Are ye not afraid of me?"

A flash of surprise widened her eyes. "Never. Why would I fear you?"

"Because I want ye. Because I am known for taking what I want."

Before she could say nay, Edan swept Lily into his arms and brought his mouth down on hers. His heart beat fiercely, and a fire unlike any he had never known swept through him at the honey taste of her lips.

Gradually, and ever so sweetly, her lips parted beneath his. *"Madness,"* a voice in his head called out. *"Madness."*

Edan struggled against a desire so fierce it frightened him in a manner he'd never been frightened before. During the bleakest moments on the battlefield and on the home front, he'd never wavered. But now...

Clasping Lilith's shoulders, he set her back from him. With his gaze riveted to hers, Edan attempted to read her thoughts whilst attempting to understand his feelings. *What in thunder had made him do that?* For a long, tense moment the agonized roar of his heart resounded in his ears.

Caught in a dark wave of confusion, he turned on his heel and stalked away. He did not want, could not have Lilith.

Silence descended on the library, broken only by echoes of footsteps and distant calls of nocturnal creatures. Darkness mitigated slightly by lantern light, a shaky light, casting shadows.

Stunned and quite speechless, Lily watched the laird leave. Edan's deep, bruising kiss had all but stopped her heart. She had never been kissed with such...gusto. But then, she'd never been kissed.

The Lady and the Laird

by

Sandra Madden

The Lady and the Laird

Cover Art by *Lisa Dawn MacDonald*

The Wild Rose Press, Inc.
PO Box 708
Adams Basin, NY 14410-0708
Visit us at www.thewildrosepress.com

Publishing History
First Edition, 2022
Trade Paperback ISBN 978-1-5092-4017-3
Digital ISBN 978-1-5092-4018-0

Published in the United States of America

Dedication

To my amazing family.
My inspiration always
is the love and laughter we share.
Plus, our love for Scotland!

Chapter 1

The Highlands, 1815

"Your bloody mad scheme cannot work," Charlotte Munro sobbed to her sister Lilith. "'Tis folly."

Lilith Munro gasped. "Bloody? Did you say bloody?"

"We shall be discovered, and Mama will marry us off to monsters. Monsters!"

Her sweet young sister had indeed said "bloody."

"I shall rue the day I ran off with you, Lily!" A ragged sob rose to a high-pitched wail.

Too late to turn back now. And you agreed to this, um, only slightly deceptive scheme.

"Dry your tears, sweet." Hurrying to her sister's side, Lily knelt beside the threadbare wing chair where her sister perched. She cupped a comforting hand against Charlotte's cool cheek. The young girl's lovely blue eyes were awash in tears. Even with her hands stuffed into the ermine muff she carried and her sky-blue pelisse fastened tightly, Charlotte shivered. Whether she shivered from fear or cold, Lily could not be certain. She could only offer words of assurance. "Do not be troubled. Mama would never think to look for us here."

At least she hoped not.

"What falsehood did you tell about how long we

would stay with the Fairlyhams following the duchess's funeral?" Charlotte sniffled, casting a deep, doubting frown at her sister.

"Never have I told a falsehood," Lily objected, "though in this instance I may have slightly misled Mama. By the by, ladies never, never use the…the word you so indelicately just—"

"You mean bloody?"

"Charlotte!" Catching herself, Lilly paused a moment to regain her composure. "You are not yourself. The journey has been too much for you." But she could not risk leaving Charlotte behind. And in truth her sister had insisted. She'd refused to be left behind. "I suggested it might be a fortnight before our return, sweet."

"Do you believe the laird will so quickly agree to your presumptuous proposal?"

"'Tis not so presumptuous. Do not be such a worrywart, Charlotte," she soothed. "All will be fine."

"When Mama discovers we have run away, and you know she will, she shall send us both to Bedlam." Charlotte heaved a shuddering sigh, looking as if she might be ill at any moment.

Bedlam remained a preferable option to Lily.

"She would do no such thing. Take several deep breaths, and you will feel better. Remaining was not an option. Would you rather be in London preparing for marriage with the old Earl of Whetfield? A wifebeater and drunkard?"

"No," she cried, the color draining from her face.

Lily stiffened, staring. "You're not going to swoon, are you?"

With a slow shake of her head, Charlotte drew in a

sob.

Not at all promising. "Please be brave, sweet."

Her frightened sister nodded but huge tears trickled down her cheeks.

Still, for all her seeming confidence, Lily was almost as worried as Charlotte. Softly humming an improvised tune, she paced. Jamie Cameron had promised to send a message to his brother Edan, the Laird of Glen Carin, announcing the Munro sisters' pending visit. A visit set in motion a little more than ten days ago in Hyde Park, when Jamie confided to Lily and Charlotte that his brother sought a wife in a marriage of convenience.

Perfect. Lily required a husband. And she also desired a marriage of convenience.

Having no time to waste, she'd made hasty, secretive plans to travel to the Highlands. Careful planning had not been an option.

"I am cold and hungry and exhausted," Charlotte whined.

"Do you wish to return home and marry old Whetfield as Mama has arranged?"

Her question was met with a new outburst of tears. "Impossible," Charlotte wailed.

Again Lily rushed to Charlotte's side. She crouched down beside her sister and clasped the young girl's hands in hers. "Besides, Glen Carin is our home…our first home. I understand you cannot remember. You were just a babe when we left. And Mama always kept you close in her chambers while father allowed me to accompany him almost everywhere."

"I promise you, there are no beasts." Lily glanced

at the fireplace. The fire slowly ebbed, along with her confidence in this admittedly daring scheme. Each never-ending minute she waited for her host, the more nervous she grew. "I should never consider marriage to a beast."

When she'd learned Edan Cameron was on the marriage market, Lily thought the situation serendipitous. She considered the laird's need an opportunity to save her sister from marriage to a man of dire reputation. At the same time, Lily would enter into a marriage of convenience with Edan she felt would be mutually beneficial to both the laird and her. 'Twas an excellent plan with no readily apparent problems. Edan, as her husband, would offer protection to Charlotte. In return, Lily would prove a most affectionate and loyal wife. Although she might have to convince Edan of that.

Sadly, she'd been too tall and too slender to have won an acceptable suitor during her three seasons. Her reddish hair and the freckles dancing across the bridge of her nose were not coveted as was Charlotte's true English beauty. Her sister's blue eyes, blond curls, and petite figure had won suitors before her first season. Now, older than most single women, Lily felt an arranged marriage the best she could do, and only to save her sister. An arranged marriage to an old friend who happened to be a respected laird was even better than she could have hoped.

Only Lily's loss of pride threatened her contrivance. Instead of her mother's solicitor bargaining with the Laird of Glen Carin, Lily must manage the marriage arrangements herself. Such a situation was neither natural nor normal. Her cheeks grew warm to even think of her audacity. Still, she must do what she must do.

"Why is the laird keeping us waiting?" Charlotte whispered. "Does he know we are here?"

"No need to whisper, sweet. You have nothing to fear here. The laird is kind but an extremely busy man."

"I hope you know…I mean you haven't seen him in years."

"Do not worry. Edan will be here very soon, and you will see his good nature for yourself. People do not change."

Lily meant to reassure herself as well as Charlotte. In fact, as she counted each passing second, Lily's dignity slipped away. A slow syrupy drip, drip, drip from a near empty bucket of pride.

Indeed. What was taking Edan so long?

Humming jauntily for Charlotte's sake, Lily crossed to the bank of tall, floor-to-ceiling windows. The drapes drawn tightly against the cold only served to create a dark and cavernous atmosphere. She threw opened the faded drapes of the nearest window. A shaft of gray light streamed into the study. Oddly, a feeling of peace settled over her as she looked out on the gray fall mist hovering over the stony hills in a melancholy cloud. 'Twas a fleeting moment before her inner turmoil once again roiled deep in her belly.

Something had gone amiss.

Something she would rather die than admit to Charlotte.

They had been kept waiting to meet the laird for far too long.

Her fingertips tingled. Her left eye twitched. She hummed.

Although she hadn't seen Edan Cameron in ten years, Lily remembered him as a strapping boy, even then as solid as an ancient oak. She recalled a handsome young man who had been kind to animals and small children. More than likely, her recollections had much to do with Lily having been a small child at the time and a constant recipient of his patience. Yet, she considered Edan a friend. She felt they shared a lifelong attachment since childhood, a connection strong enough to endure long periods of separation.

Of course, she worried. She might be romanticizing a relationship that only existed in her mind.

Her eye twitched once again serving to remind her that she had no control over her nerves or her twitch.

"What…what if the laird has already found a wife and married?" Charlotte asked.

The same dreadful thought had occurred to Lily several times as well during their journey. But she'd stubbornly pushed the troubling scenario out of her mind. "Not to worry, we shall employ my contingency plan." *Although her contingency plan to find the Doonie Purse was little more than an airy hope. Certainly a more realistic plan would occur to her if further planning proved necessary. She could not rely on a fairy tale.*

Just as she was about to take up pacing and humming again, heavy, commanding footsteps echoed in the corridor just outside the door. Growing louder as they drew closer.

"Someone's coming," Charlotte hissed.

"There is no reason to be afraid. Smile, sweet."

With nerves ajangle, Lily pinched her cheeks and squared her shoulders to stand frozen in military-like attention. Her hands trembled in anxious expectation. The moment grew near, the moment she'd both feared and anticipated since making the decision to return to Glen Carin.

Her mouth went dry. *Oh, no!*

She would not be able to speak a word. She swallowed to wet her throat. She swallowed again. And then, her fears…vanished. Along with every thought. Her mind went blank.

Edan Cameron burst through the double doors and strode past Lily and Charlotte without so much of a glance. In less time than it took Lily to blink, Edan's tall, muscular figure filled the room, an indomitable force seeming to steal every particle of available oxygen and leaving her inexplicably breathless. He stalked into the room making his way toward the large mahogany desk where Rob Munro had once sat.

Charlotte sucked in a shaky breath.

Transfixed, Lily seemed unable to do even that. She stared. Unbecoming for an English lady. Magnificent. The boy she remembered had become a magnificent man. An intimidating man.

Edan towered over most mortals. Dressed in black trousers, he wore a white full-sleeved, laced linen shirt of the type she envisioned a poet to wear, and black, mud-caked boots. The laird might easily have been mistaken for an English country gentleman. But Lily knew better. A chill spiraled down her spine followed by a strange flutter of her heart. She understood the laird could be a dark and dangerous man. He'd not been raised to be a gentleman. He'd been raised to become a fearsome warrior. As the leader of his clan, he was, and would always be, a lionhearted Highlander.

The trembling of her hands intensified, even as she reached out to steady herself on the back of Charlotte's chair. Edan's furrowed brow indicated the interruption necessitated by her arrival had caused him great annoyance. A knot the size of London Bridge twisted in the pit of Lily's stomach. He might very well be a beast.

Once behind the desk, Edan raised his head. His gaze locked on hers.

A bolt of heat shot like lightning straight down to her toes. To curl her toes. To steal her breath away.

Unable to tear her gaze from his, Lily watched in silent fascination as his irritated expression gave way to puzzlement. His dark indigo-blue eyes flashed with wariness, but not of recognition. His questioning gaze drifted to Charlotte whose complexion had become as white as winter snow.

Lowering her eyes, Lily dipped a swift, wobbly curtsy.

Edan's deep voice rumbled as he gave her a sharp, "Good day."

She raised her chin. "Good day, Your Grace."

"Yer Grace?" He stared for a long moment before speaking, "Begging yer pardon, but dinna ken ye?"

Lily stood immobilized as a cold wave of crushing disappointment rushed through her. New fears quickly followed. For the life of her, she could not catch her breath. 'Twas apparent that Edan had not been informed of her visit. And while she did not expect him to recognize Charlotte, she could not believe he did not recognize her! "Do you not remember me? Us?" she blurted.

Running a hand through his dark hair, he further

disheveled the stray blue-black locks which had come loose from the leather strip and fell to his broad shoulders. His perplexed frown deepened as he studied her through a narrowed, steely-eyed gaze. "Nay," he said at last, shaking his head. "I would have remembered bedding such bonnie lasses."

Charlotte let out a small squeaky whimper.

"No. No b-bedding." Lily's lips quivered as she shot him what she hoped to be a wider, brighter smile, the smile of a confident woman. Confidence she absolutely did not feel.

He met her smile with a slow shake of his head, the sign of an obviously baffled man. "Nay?"

"You jest," she said, raising her voice.

"I never jest." He folded his arms across his sizable chest. "I ken ye, yet no' in the biblical way?"

"Aye." The affirmative word said so often in her youth slipped as easily from her tongue like silk, as if she'd been using the Gaelic declaration all of her life.

"Aye?" One dark brow shot up. The striking laird and chief of his clan appeared incredulous.

"Aye." Mild irritation warring within her, Lily waited in the unsettling silence that followed. A flicker of light at last flashed in Edan's stormy-sea eyes. She could not prevent the spread of a small smile as she watched recognition slowly dawn in his expression.

His eyes grew wider before his intense gaze narrowed on her once again. His voice dropped to a hoarse whisper. "Lilith?"

A lump lodged in her throat. Tears rushed up to settle behind her eyes. Unable to speak, she simply nodded. He'd called her Lilith. She hadn't been called by her rightful name in years. The memory of her

9

childhood name warmed her. His voice, deep and soft, curled round her heart like a lover's embrace. Or had she only imagined the affection held in her name?

"Lilith Munro, is it ye?"

Drat the demon imagination!

"Aye," she replied, fighting back the unexpected tears and forcing a smile. She hoped he could not see the maddening way her lips quivered. "'Tis I."

"Lilith!" He repeated her given name yet again in deep rumbling tones of shock and—dare she think it—delight. "Nay!"

'Twas not delight she heard.

"Aye? Truly? Lilith?" Edan regarded her with an expression of wonder, shaking his head as if completely dumbfounded. "'Tis been a long time, little Lilith. I dinna think to ever see ye again." His lilting Scottish burr gave his speech the rhythm of a song.

Lily continued to smile like the idiot child she used to be. When they were youngsters, Edan's family owned the neighboring farm of Cameron Castle. From the time she'd been a wee eight-year-old lass and Edan a strapping lad of sixteen, she had adored the tall, dark warrior.

The rugged Highlander's appearance hadn't changed so very much, except for the savage scar that slashed across his left cheek. Strangely enough, Edan's battle scar added an element of danger and...and excitement to his countenance.

He came around the desk in several swift strides and gathered Lily into his arms. She experienced unexpected pleasure in his welcoming embrace, in the heat of his hard Highlander body. Her heart raced as if it might burst from her chest.

"No need to stand on ceremony when a bonnie lass returns, no?" He flashed a grin before settling her back, and then his grin slid quickly away. Goose bumps rose on her arms. He might be a ruthless rogue and battle-worn warrior, but he was a handsome devil. His grin could melt the heart of a stone.

"No. No need. But I am not the lass you remember."

With a growl of frustration, Edan took both her hands in his, "Let me look at ye."

His hands, large, warm and calloused, enveloped hers, causing Lily's pulse to skip. His gaze quickly skimmed the length of her, almost as if he were embarrassed to scrutinize her so.

But she felt no embarrassment. She wanted him to see her, really see her as the woman she'd become. "I am a proper English lady now. Is it not astonishing?" she teased.

"Aye." One side of his mouth hitched up in a slightly wicked half-smile. "Astonishing indeed. Ye have grown into a beautiful woman, Lilith Munro."

She was caught off guard by his quiet compliment. A warm tingle skipped down her spine. "I...I was only a child of ten when I left the Highlands," she reminded him. Her voice cracked with unexpected emotion. When her mother forced Lily to leave Glen Carin and all she had ever known, her heart had been broken.

"And now ye are grown," he stated the obvious in the same soft tone. With each passing minute, the hard planes of Edan's face appeared to relax. "I dinna recognize ye withoot a smudge of dirt on yer cheek and yer hair being all wild from running with the wind," he said, releasing her hands.

Edan not only teased her then as he did now, he'd been the only male for miles around who took the time to notice her. When she had been all arms and legs and general gawkiness, it was Edan who'd taught her how to fish and how to aim a bow and arrow with deadly precision. Skills she had not required at Almacks. Skills she took pride in, nonetheless.

His questioning gaze drifted to Charlotte, whose complexion had become as white as winter snow. "And who might this bonnie lass be?"

"My sister, Charlotte."

"Aaah, the bairn Charlotte?"

Charlotte cast a tremulous smile his way before lowering her eyes.

Lily spoke quickly. "My sister is fragile and excessively tired from our journey. If she could rest…"

"At once," he interrupted. "Ye must think me a sorry host." Edan pulled the nearest bell rope.

In a matter of minutes, the sturdy, sour-faced woman who had guided Charlotte and Lily to the study earlier arrived.

"Netta is my housekeeper," he told Charlotte. "She'll show ye to a bedchamber."

"Thank you…" Rising, she made a swift curtsey and turned away. Head lowered, Charlotte looked disturbingly like a lamb being led to slaughter as she followed the glum housekeeper out of the study.

"I will join you directly," Lily called after her sister. *Please do not weep.*

"And ye, Lilith? Do you no' need to rest?"

She turned back to Edan with a smile. "Nay. I have waited a long time to speak with you."

"Aye?"

She noted a wariness to his question, but rushed to complete what she had been practicing in her head every day on the journey to Glen Carin. In truth, Lily had much to say. "Since last we met, I have become a lady in every sense."

Although her mother might disagree.

His dark brows slashed near to meeting. To Lily's dismay, Edan regarded her with undisguised skepticism. "Aye?"

What had she done to earn his distrust? She forged ahead. "In London, I am addressed as Lady Lilith."

"Lady? Have ye been to finishing school then?"

She grinned. "Do I not look finished?"

"Aye." Although he did not appear amused, Edan nodded. "Finished indeed."

Smiling sweetly, she dipped her head.

But the laird's eyes darkened as he looked past her and about the chamber. His jaw tightened. "Is Lady Frances…"

Lily interrupted before he could finish the question. "No." She understood Edan's concern and rushed to assure him. "My mother did not accompany us. But our maids, an outrider and two footmen have traveled with Charlotte and me to ensure our safety."

"A regular entourage," he said with a quirk of his lips. "But no' to worry. I am certain we have room for all." His expression darkened once again as his gaze narrowed on Lily. "I confess I am surprised Lady Frances allowed ye to make such an arduous journey with only yer servants."

"Do you not find life full of surprises?" Lily quickly changed the subject rather than confess to Edan she had told her mother a small white lie in order to escape Lady Frances's objection.

"Aye, but only to ye will I admit Lady Frances frightened me more than any enemy I ever encountered on the battlefield."

"Over the years, I've gained courage when dealing with Mama. I have managed to pull the wool over her eyes so that she believes me to be a proper young lady."

"Eh? Proper?"

"Almost always," she teased with a smile. Lily noticed the laird's Highland burr slipped in and out during their conversation. He'd spent too much time with the British to play the middling Scot farmer.

Like a man awakening from a deep sleep, Edan shook his head slowly. "I canna get over the change in ye."

"I am almost as tall as you," Lily said with a hint of pride, although she disliked her height the way some women disliked the size of their nose or the set of their mouth. In truth, Edan stood a good head taller than she, a fact she appreciated. "I am not the midge you once called me."

He cocked his head to one side and flipped back the midnight lock that fell across his brow. "A midge?"

As a youngster, harboring a devoted but well-hidden, she believed, affection for Edan, she'd cried when he compared her to the tiny insect that drove many a person mad. But he could make the comparison no longer. Lily stood as tall as most men now at five-feet, eight inches, much too tall to strike a damsel-in-distress pose. She thought her appearance more closely resembled that of the mythical Amazon women. However, on a positive note, her height had thus far saved her from Lady Frances's marriage schemes. No wealthy member of the English aristocracy had expressed a desire to marry the ton's tallest woman. She remained, at twenty-four years of age, unwed and considered a spinster by most.

Lily knew well her tall, slender form proved a source of angst to her mother. Lady Frances never let her forget that beauty in London, perhaps in all of Great Britain, was measured by the petite round figures of her peers, exemplified by the conventional beauty possessed by Charlotte.

"Nay! I never called ye a midge," Edan protested.

The laird's objection jolted Lily out of her reverie.

"You did indeed and perhaps for good cause. But I promise I am no longer the little girl with a penchant for stealing horses from the stable for unchaperoned rides."

His horse in particular.

Edan's smile dissolved. "A little hellion ye were."

She waggled her index finger in disagreement. "Impetuous."

His lips tightened. "Mulish."

"Determined," she countered.

"Incorrigible."

"Adventuresome," Lily insisted, enjoying the way he rolled his r's.

At last, one corner of Edan's mouth hitched up in a rueful smile. "Our memories differ."

"My father called me his princess."

"Yer father had a blind eye when it came to ye."

She smiled. "Perhaps."

"Rob Munro was a good man."

"Aye." she whispered. The memory of her father always brought a smile to her lips and pain to her heart.

She missed him still. She would always miss him.

"Rob Munro's bairns returned to the Highlands." Wonder etched Edan's tone. "When my housekeeper, Netta, told me a stranger waited in my study, an old friend, I dinna think of ye."

"Did Jamie not send you a message that Charlotte and I would be making a visit to Glen Carin?"

Dismissing his brother Jamie with a derisive grunt, the striking laird answered, "I've not heard from my brother since he led the drovers with our cattle to London. 'Twas weeks past."

"I see." Lily's mild reply concealed her annoyance. She would wring Jamie's neck if ever she came upon him again. "In that case I must apologize for my intrusion."

"Och!" Shaking his head, Edan took her hand and led her to one of the wing-backed chairs that flanked the fireplace. "'Tis no intrusion and it is I who should apologize for my bad manners. Ye have taken me by surprise."

A man who did not welcome surprises, as Lily remembered.

"Sit by the fire. I am curious as to how ye came upon Jamie and why ye have come to visit the Highlands."

As Edan stoked the fire, Lily noted the worn burgundy fabric of the gilt Hepplewhite chairs that gave evidence the furniture had been in service since she had lived in Glen Carin. Her father spent a fortune importing the finest English furniture for her mother, for which he received little appreciation.

Sucking in a nervous breath, Lily shook off old unpleasant memories and returned her thoughts to the present. Foremost, she took pleasure in the increased heat of the fire. At last she could remove her pelisse. The forest green wool garment was heavy with travel dust.

Edan helped her, tossing the cloak aside to the settee.

Lily sat primly in one of the two chairs flanking the fireplace. "I met Jamie quite by accident while riding with Charlotte in Hyde Park." she told Edan, smiling as she recalled her unexpected meeting with the devilish Jamie Cameron. He remained dear to her even though the youngest Cameron had proven he could not be relied upon. "He promised to send you a message that I would be coming ho…" Lily paused, and then rushed on to cover her slip. Glen Carin was no longer her home. "…to Glen Carin."

Edan sank into the chair opposite her. Lily watched as the chair disappeared beneath his huge warrior frame. Upon hearing the furniture legs squeak, she half expected the old chair to give way. "I received no message."

"I apologize…"

"No need. I'll wait to hear from my brother as to just why he was riding in Hyde Park instead of attending to business," Edan said. "Jamie will spin a fine tale, I ken. But I eagerly await his explanation as to why, although he had time to ride in the park, he could not find the time to send me a message that ye would be visiting." He shook his head in the manner of one despairing. "My young brother is a rogue if ever there was one. If he doesn't return soon with our profits from the cattle sale, I shall personally hang him by his heels."

As swift as a lightning bolt, Lily was struck once

by a horrid, skin-crawling thought. Her eye twitched, not once but twice. What else had young Jamie gotten wrong? Did Edan truly desire a wife? Was he indeed interested in a marriage of convenience? Worse, had he already wed?

"Y…you must think me rude beyond belief for appearing without warning," she stuttered.

"Nay. Nay," he repeated in a less convincing tone. "Not yer doing. But tell me, why ye have come back to Glen Carin?"

Courage eluded her. Robbed her of speech for a long moment. She batted her eyes to cover the near-constant twitch and thick silence. "I, I have missed the, the lochs and the glens. I have missed the thistles and bluebells." Lily paused, stalling with a smile. He'd think her a featherbrain. And at the moment she felt like one. She could tell Edan the truth and die of mortification before she took her next breath or tell the handsome laird a small white lie and leave Glen Carin with a bit of her pride intact. But her white lies were accumulating. Soon she would be unable to remember them all or to whom she'd told them. She was becoming increasingly uncomfortable with how quickly she resorted to a small twist of the truth.

Taking a deep, steadying breath, Lily straightened her shoulders and directed her gaze straight into his eyes. "I have returned…returned…" Her voice trailed off as resolve deserted her.

"Aye?" he prompted, his expression bordering on impatience.

A sudden, unwelcome thought occurred to her. *What if Edan indeed had become a Highlander beast in the years between then and now? It made no matter.*

She must do what she must do—for Charlotte.

"Have ye lost yer voice? Ye never had trouble before as I remember it. Ye had plenty to say."

"I do. I mean…" she averted her gaze from his. A dark unsettling gaze. "I understand you are interested in a marriage of convenience."

Edan started. His brows met in a deep frown. "Do ye no'?"

She dared not stop. "As I also wish to enter a marriage of convenience, the journey to Glen Carin seemed logical. At the risk of you thinking me to be quite shameless, I have come to offer a proposal."

"A proposal?" he repeated in what sounded very much like a growl. A warning growl.

"I would be greatly honored to b-become your wife."

The laird's jaw dropped. His eyes widened.

"If you will have me in a marriage of convenience," she added quietly.

Lily had rendered the mighty-sized man speechless. The heat of a blush singed her cheeks, but emboldened by Edan's temporary inertia, Lily continued, "Jamie mentioned you are in need of a wife, and he has dedicated himself to arranging a proper marriage for you. He confided that you are too busy rebuilding the estate to properly court a woman. Jamie suggested I might make a welcome…ah, acceptable…candidate."

Edan's eyes appeared to have glazed over. He nodded slowly and fixed his obviously troubled gaze on her. Or was it anger she saw in his eyes? "My eejit brother made that suggestion to ye, did he?"

"Aye," she croaked.

"'Tis true I asked Jamie to investigate a marriage of convenience, but I dinna give him leave to become the town crier."

"He only meant to help you. Believe me, 'tis mortifying for me to propose marriage to…for myself." The words stuck in her throat resulting again in the embarrassing croaking sound. Still, she persevered in a tumble of words, fearing if she stopped now, she would be unable to continue. "I know 'tis a parent or solicitor's task to arrange a marriage. You might well think me shameless, but no. I promise you I am not. While I understand how audacious arranging my own marriage might seem…I, I believe you and I would get along famously, and it is my fondest hope you will consider my proposal."

The flummoxed laird hunched forward, laying his forearms to rest on his muscled thighs. His dark brows dipped toward his nose, a noble nose set in a rugged, sun-darkened complexion. As Edan leaned toward her, the laces of his shirt widened to expose a dusting of coal black chest curls.

Without warning, Lily's heart skipped a precious beat. She quickly averted her gaze from his chest. She found safety in the serious contemplation of his boots, scuffed and caked with dirt. The boots of a working man.

Her heart resumed its natural beat.

"Lilith. Ye pay me a great compliment." Edan wore a somber expression as he reached out and placed a hand lightly on her arm. A large warm hand.

She breathed in his scent, an oddly intoxicating mixture of leather, earth and man. "I beg you not to hasten in your answer, Edan. I realize I have shocked and surprised you. You may wish to have time to think about my…my proposition before you reply."

"I confess, ye have—"

"There is joy in an arranged marriage. Such a marriage provides a freedom of sorts, a partnership without emotional entanglements. If we owned an inn, we should be partners. I would be the cook and you would be the keeper. The innkeeper."

"Lilith, you make a fine argument for—"

"Love can be so complicated. We have history, you and me. We are friends, so there is no need for anything more."

"I understand that you—"

"Oh, 'tis true, 'twould be preferable to become better acquainted again," Lily hastily interrupted once again, unwilling to allow Edan rejecting her proposal out of hand. "In any event, my sister and I shall require several days of rest before returning to London. Perhaps we can become reacquainted during that time…unless you would rather have us leave on the morrow."

"Nay, nay, lass. Ye shall stay and rest, of course. Ye are welcome at Glen Carin as long as you require. What sort of brute do ye take me for?"

"Not a brute. You were always kind to me when I was a child." *Although he might have become a brute in the intervening years, for all she knew.*

"Aye, when ye were no more than a bairn," he repeated. "It pleases me that kindly 'tis how ye remember me."

"I am a woman now." Lily had made her decision. Beast or brute, she must win him.

She stood straight and tall, raising her head high so Edan might take her full measure. Smiling down upon him, she sighed a bit plaintively. "And I appreciate kindness in a Highlander even more."

A plainly confused expression played on the laird's strong features. "A woman…indeed."

While Lily had no actual training in the art of seduction, she refused to abandon her plan. Nothing had changed. He had not denied his need for a wife. He had not refused her proposal, nor had he agreed to her proposition. She meant to spend the next several days charming the laird with all the womanly wiles she possessed. Apparently, Edan still required a wife, and in order to save Charlotte, she absolutely needed a husband as soon as possible. How difficult could it be to come to terms?

The fire crackled. The dim light darkened. Pine-scented smoke from the fireplace stole through the closed chamber. The silence was deafening.

****

Edan Cameron had not doubted Lilith's womanly attributes from the first moment he'd entered the study and set eyes on her. He had been captivated—before he'd recognized her as the devil-child grown, at which point he'd found himself at a loss for words.

'Twas one of the few moments of his life he'd been struck speechless. The other came shortly afterward, when she proposed an arranged marriage with him. Not only had he never expected to see Lilith again in this lifetime, he'd never expected the skinny, mischievous child he had known to become such a beauty. Edan suspected her wide jewel-green eyes and mass of thick copper locks had made many an Englishman in London do silly things in hopes of winning her favor. But he knew her better. He knew the true nature hidden beneath Lilith's beguiling features. Still, he'd experienced some amazement. Who would have guessed the little rapscallion lass would blossom into a fair-skinned beauty with tempting, pouty pink lips?

And who would have thought she'd undertake a dangerous journey for the sole purpose of proposing marriage to him? Indeed, 'twas scandalous behavior. Even for her.

He suspected she'd been involved in more than one scandalous situation and disgraced herself. 'Twas the only reason a beautiful woman would run off to the Highlands to propose marriage to a veritable stranger. As in the past, Lilith had no shame, and even if she possessed a modicum of pride, a "lady" was not the sort of woman he wished to marry. He required an industrious Highland woman who knew how to work and did not mind getting her hands dirty or her gown mussed.

Lily broke the tense silence, interrupting his thoughts. "Edan, I must confess, I have missed the Highlands…and I have missed you."

Missed plaguing him to death, more likely.

Eager to end the unsettling conversation, Edan rose. Raising her hand to his lips, he brushed her soft skin with a light kiss. "I am glad to see ye, Lilith. I look forward to learning how ye have spent these last…how many years?"

A golden light twinkled deep within her meadow green eyes as she gazed into his. "Near ten years."

"Ten." He repeated with a shake of his head. "We may require days rather than hours to reminisce."

Why had he proposed days? He had not meant days. Mere seconds more would suffice.

"I am certain we shall." Her pouty lips curved into a kissable smile. "Days, perhaps even months will be required."

Months? Unthinkable! A kissable smile? Was he going mad?

No. However he did need time to solve the conundrum she'd presented. How to refuse her proposal without further discredit to her? He did not wish to hurt her unduly. She was Rob Munro's daughter after all. But he must send Lily back to London as quickly as possible.

He swept a hand through his hair. "We'll sup together this evening."

Much to his chagrin, her smile brightened the room. "I would like that."

"Until then, I must see to matters of utmost importance awaiting my attention. Netta will prepare a chamber for ye."

"I appreciate your thoughtfulness. As a young man you were always kind to me, Edan."

Kind? She recalled him as being kind to her? In the past, he'd had no choice in the matter whenever he could not avoid her. His father would have given him a proper beating had he acted on his impulses regarding the hellion.

"Yer memory serves me well, Lilith."

If only his memory served her as well. Unfortunately, it did not. Arranged or no', Hell would freeze over before he married Lilith Munro!

Chapter 2

Edan Cameron had gained a reputation as a man who planned. He strategized on the battlefield and on the home front. He devised a backup plan for every possible scenario. With the possible exception of "surprises." Trained as a warrior, he'd gained firsthand experience in battle, the sort that flared between clans and those that arose between nations. He'd always been in command. He issued orders. Obey or be dispatched. But he always had been a gentleman in the drawing room. Today he'd been sorely tested, but his manners triumphed in the end.

As Edan made his way to the stables, thoughts of the young girl he'd known swirled through his head. Much as he hated to admit it, the gangly daughter of Rob Munro, who once seemed to take pleasure in following closely on his heels with the sole purpose of tormenting him, had grown into a beautiful woman, if a little long in the tooth.

Her long dark lashes were most astonishing, and Edan had not missed the gleam of intelligence, nor the unexpected glint of intuitiveness reflected in her eyes. Lilith Munro possessed enough extraordinary physical features to make a mortal man wary.

Edan's silent ruminations gave way to an unplanned snort. As one who had witnessed her riding through the moors like a wild child, he could not believe her claim to have become a lady. Highly unlikely!

Following the end of the war, a survivor of the Battle of Waterloo, Edan had returned to the Highlands to restore his name and the land of his clan. Lilith Munro had no part in his plans. Aye, he wanted a wife. He meant to marry a plain and simple woman who did not fear getting her hands dirty or mind cleaning a barn. This strong Scot woman who he hadn't yet met would help restore the manor, prepare his meals and give him an heir.

Striding quickly to the stables, he pushed all thoughts of his unexpected guests to the back of his mind. He had no time for guests. He'd been about to ride out to check on the new flock of Blackface sheep when he'd received the news of a visitor, the arrival of an old friend. But Lilith had never been a friend of his; she'd been more like an itchy rash he'd been unable to scratch.

Spotting his brother waiting for him outside the stables, Edan hurried forward.

"What took ye away?" Angus asked.

Angus Cameron, taller and broader, and two years younger than Edan, lived at Castle Cameron with their brother Finlay. The castle, also in disrepair, adjoined the Glen Carin property and was the true Cameron ancestral home.

The big, rusty-bearded man swung a meaty leg over his mount even as Edan hoisted himself up on the glossy back of his big black gelding, Dragon.

"We have unexpected guests."

"And who would be arriving unannounced no'?"

"Lilith Munro," he said quietly, letting the name

linger on his tongue.

"Lilith Munro?" Angus repeated, his ginger brows rising high on his broad forehead. "I canna believe it."

"Lilith and her sister, Charlotte. Jamie was to send a message that they would be arriving at Glen Carin for a…visit."

"Aaah." Angus leaned back in his saddle with a wag of his head as if Edan's simple declaration explained everything. "But Jamie dinna send the message."

"No." Grumbling, Edan nudged his horse forward. "However, he did remember my wish to make a marriage arrangement in all due haste."

"Ye asked us all to keep an eye oot for a good match."

"A good match, aye, which mind ye, would eliminate Lilith! Jamie confided my wishes to Lilith. Of all the women in the United Kingdom, she would be the last I would wed." Edan vowed he would rather abandon everything he owned and sail to North America rather than take a known minx like Lilith as his wife. "I'll have Jamie's haid on a spike."

"Has the lass grown ugly, no?" Angus asked his voice low and heavy with suspicion.

"Appearance means naught. Lilith has the soft, fragile hands of a woman who has never lifted more than a fork."

"A lady's hands?"

"Aye. But she is no lady despite her claim. Angus, always remember, a tiger canna change its stripes. Lilith was a she-devil and more than likely remains so. Age does not change a person's essential nature, not a woman not a man."

"I dinna—"

"Do you not remember how she tortured us when we were young? Have ye forgotten how she stole my favorite horse from the stable during a visit with her father? She could have injured my mare. And herself," he added as an afterthought.

Angus nodded his head in a slow, sage-like agreement. "Oh, aye, a wee mischievous one, lass Lilith was. All spunk and spirit, no?"

Edan gave a grunt in reply. "I shall never forget or forgive her for the time she stole my trousers while I swam in the loch. The brat hid my garments and watched me while bare as a newborn babe I searched for my trousers and shirt."

Angus chuckled. "Aye, playful one, she was."

"Playful!"

"'Tis the way I thought of her." He shrugged. "But much can be forgiven a bonnie lass. If she is bonnie. Is Lilith bonnie?"

Clenching his jaw, Edan refused to answer, fresh anger adding more fuel to his fire. "And another thing. Lady Frances. Can you imagine having such a shrew for a mother-in-law? Och! The woman would drain every half-penny from my pockets."

Angus responded with a start and an anxious frown. "Has Lady Frances come with Lilith?"

"Nay, she and her sister have come alone. Lady Frances remains in England—where she belongs. And Lilith too."

Angus pulled up on his reins. "I should greet the lass. I canna have Lilith think me rude."

"No." Slowing his steed, Edan shook his head. "Do nothing to encourage the hoyden."

"Dinna seem right."

"She's resting from the journey, and we have business to attend."

"Are you certain Lilith traveled all this way to marry ye?"

"The brazen lass proposed to me!"

"Aye, that would seem serious. Lilith and the laird. Man and wife," he mused.

"Never," Edan growled. But with the seed planted, he thought of what it might be like to find Lily waiting in the drawing room every evening. He envisioned her tall and regal with rosy begged-to-be-kissed lips and sparkling emerald eyes that shone only for him. The vision caused his heart to pound against his chest, swift and strong. Odd.

"How terrible could it be?"

"Vera terrible! Who, I ask ye, but a reckless woman would make the dangerous journey from London to Glen Carin with her young sister, their maids, an outrider and two footmen? She's not changed," Edan grumbled.

"Bah! Little Lilith had a sweetness aboot her…as well as the devil."

Eden remembered. He knew as a young girl Lilith had never been like most females. Sensitive she was to others and what they were feeling, when she wasn't making trouble. She'd been a wee bit eccentric as well. Some believed eccentricity lived only within the elderly. But he knew better. "Och! Angus, yer memory dinna serve."

"Mayhap. I dinna recall the young sister at all."

"Charlotte was a bairn when Lady Frances sold our father Glen Carin and left the Highlands."

Angus nodded his head in understanding. "Is she an imp as well?"

"Nay. Charlotte appears to be an innocent, a sweet young lass vera unlike Lilith."

"Are you believin' Lilith to be a desperate woman, then?"

"Desperate. Aye. If ever a woman was born to plague a man, 'tis Lilith."

"Has she returned to the Highlands to stay, do ye suppose?" Angus asked before answering his own question. "Ye know a lass born in the Highlands canna stay away."

"Put Lilith out of yer head, Angus." Edan meant to do the same, eliminating the *lady* from his thoughts. She did not fool him for a moment. He knew the real Lilith Munro. Still, memories of a young, slightly wild Lilith taking him by surprise momentarily chased away the worries and brought a smile to his lips. Worse, for no good reason his body heated as if he'd been standing too near a raging fire, a fire ignited by the graceful curves and bright eyes of the woman she'd become.

"I will reject her proposal."

"Aye?" His brother sounded puzzled even after Edan's logical explanations.

"I have more important matters on my mind."

"Then I shall marry Lilith," Angus declared.

"Dinna think it. 'Tis time now to see if Brodie made good on his threat to slay our new sheep."

"Aye." But evidently Angus's thoughts remained on their unexpected guest. "I'll bring out me pipe and play for Lilith and her sister tonight."

"Not tonight." His burly brother only imagined he played the bagpipe well. Edan's head ached every time

Angus played.

"I'll ask the lady, and if Lilith wishes me to play, I'll play," he argued.

"Let's ride. I'm anxious to see a full herd of sheep."

"We've had no message from Finn of any problems."

"No news dinnae ease my mind. Brodie is a cunning one."

"Aye, he mistakes cunning for intelligence."

Edan nodded his agreement. Intelligence triumphed over cunning every time. His intelligence would see the cunning Lilith racing back to London before the next full moon.

His clan and Brodie's had been feuding for months and he meant to put an end to it. Ranulf Brodie owned the farmland to the south and had made it plain on every occasion that he would not tolerate sheep grazing near his property. Edan was determined to turn a goodly number of his fields into grazing pastures. Blackface sheep were the future of Scotland and raising the animals was the best way to turn a profit, along with a herd of the strong, shaggy-haired, rust-colored cattle.

His irritation spiked. Now, in addition to protecting his clan and sheep from Brodie's wrath, he also had Lilith Munro and her sister to protect. Och!

****

Lily's proposal to the laird had not gone well. If she had persuaded him, Edan would not have left her so quickly. Without an answer. Her heart weighed heavily within in her chest. Disappointment flowed through her veins, followed by determination. She would not give up. She refused to give up.

Although she could not claim to be a ravishing beauty like Charlotte, neither was she unattractive. Her stomach tossed with yet another bout of nerves. Lily dared not think Edan would refuse her proposal.

"I am intelligent, loyal…and patient." She silently recited her attributes to herself. No, if she were to be honest, she was not always patient. She allowed herself a deep sigh.

When Edan's housekeeper at last arrived, she followed Netta from the study. The silent woman owned a squat solid figure and kept a hurried pace, which caused the folds beneath her chin to jiggle in a disturbing way. With her chapped lips tightly set and her cold, muddy-brown eyes focused straight ahead, Netta bustled up the stairs and down the chilly stone corridors of the second-floor bedchambers. As a child, Lily had run down this same corridor many times, losing the ribbons from her hair, and sometimes losing her slippers.

The second floor of Glen Carin Manor held ten bedchambers, most with sitting rooms and occupying both the east and west wing. The manor had been designed to accommodate dozens of guests from as far as London and as near as Stirling. At the start of her marriage, Lady Frances planned to host summer house parties and fall hunting parties that would lure her aristocratic London friends to the Highlands. Her mother's plans appeared to have failed because Lily could not recall any large parties held in her Highland home.

Charlotte had been too young to remember, but life changed when their dear father fell ill. Lily's heart slowly broke as she watched her da die a bit each day.

From a strong, broad-shouldered Scotsman who could balance the weight of the world on his shoulders, he withered away to skin and bones without the strength to leave his bed. Rob Munro was a poet, a *filidh*, quite unlike the chief and warrior he had been born to be. He read and wrote and possessed a good and generous heart, a heart as big as Loch Ness. Unfortunately, his kindness was often mistaken for weakness or lack of intelligence. Lily knew differently.

Day after day, Lily sat and read to him. She listened to his stories about the Doonies when he felt able to tell a tale. She held his hands and rubbed his arms as the life slipped away from him in the early morning hours of a bleak winter morning.

"The Doonie Purse," her father had whispered just before he died. "'Tis here in the Highlands and will sustain you, my dear, when I canna be near."

At the time, she'd considered his mumblings the result of a feverish mind. But quite unexpectedly, his words returned to her in quiet moments. In reflection, it made sense that her da would have known a time would come when his children would need protection from the will of Lady Frances. Perhaps he'd left a Doonie Purse in Glen Carin to provide that protection.

According to Scottish legend, the Doonie was a shape-shifting Scot fairy able to take the form of a pony, an old man, or an old woman. The fanciful myth also promised the Doonie's purse contained untold treasure.

She might not believe in fairies or shape shifters, and certainly her father had not. But the more she thought on it, the more she felt a purse might indeed exist. Rob Munro knew his spendthrift English wife could not hold on to as much as a farthing. A Doonie Purse left by her da might contain the funds to save Charlotte from a dreadful marriage. 'Twas something, a bit of hope to fall back on if Lily's scheme failed and marriage with Edan eluded her.

When her mother, in an unprecedented move that set tongues wagging, sold Glen Carin to Edan's father, Lily was unable to protest. Too young, she had no choice but to obey her mother. Rob Munro was not yet cold in his grave when Lady Frances whisked a heartbroken Lily and her young sister Charlotte back to London. Lily cried constantly while Lady Frances appeared giddy with happiness. Her mother could not wait to once again take her place in London society. Civilized society, as she often pointed out.

Lily had been surprised by the stab of melancholy which pierced her heart when she first set eyes on the huge stone manor house when they rode up this morning. Glen Carin, the Highland home of her youth, located just northeast of Perthshire in the rocky hills and craggy spills of Scotland, remained just as she remembered.

Her musings ended when at last the housekeeper stopped and opened the latch of a heavily carved door. She stood aside for Lily to enter the blue bedchamber. Or so it had been called when she was a young girl. Blue had faded to gray.

"Yer trunks have been brought up an yer sister waits in the chamber next to this un." Netta told her, in a snappish tone. "Willna be anythin' else?"

"A bath and a cup of tea would be lovely." Lily was anxious to wash away the dust and grime from her journey.

Netta frowned and exerted more energy than required to close the door behind her.

Lily sighed. One more soul to win over.

But first to see and comfort her sister. Lily knocked on the adjoining door and opened it at the same time. "Charlotte?"

The drapes were drawn, and the chamber lay in shadow. Charlotte rested on the bed, the back of one hand to her forehead. "I wish to be alone."

"Would you like me to have your supper served here in your bedchamber?"

"Yes, though I shall not be able to swallow a thing. My head aches and my stomach tumbles. I wish to return to London immediately. This has been a dreadful mistake."

"Impossible, sweet. We must stay and see my plan through. You shall feel better in the morning."

"I doubt it. The laird strikes me as an angry giant rather than good-natured landowner."

"Perhaps Edan's anger comes from when he was a boy. Da once confided in me that Edan's father beat him unmercifully, leaving horrid scars on his back. Do not judge a man you do not know."

"I know you cannot marry him, Lily."

"I can and I will." She shot her sister a forced smile. "The laird has many attributes. Did you not notice how handsome he is?"

"A handsome appearance will not last."

When did her sister get so wise?

"I'll look in on you after I have supped with Edan."

Charlotte's deep sigh could have shaken the walls were they less strong. "Do not worry over me."

"I shall not. Clara will take exceedingly good care

of you." Lily said. Charlotte's maid Clara behaved more like a hovering nanny. "Cheer up, sweet." Shooting her sister an encouraging smile, Lily retreated to her own chamber.

Several hours later, bathed, rested, and refreshed, Lily took care to dress carefully for supper with Edan. She and Charlotte had traveled with just one trunk each to keep their mother from becoming suspicious. A funeral did not require more than one trunk. From the limited selection, Lily chose a shimmering silk Empire gown in the light mint green shade of summer past. Wide fabric roses in the same silky material trimmed the hem, the capped sleeves, and the wide strip of ribbon beneath her breasts.

Lady Frances indulged herself and her daughters with the finest fashion money could purchase, from the most sought-after seamstresses and milliners to be found in London. Appearances meant everything to her mother even in the face of dwindling finances. She shared her belief with her daughters often. "You cannot attract a worthy suitor if you are dressed in rags."

Rummaging through her velvet lined jewel box, she set aside two old wooden keys resting among the baubles while she withdrew small emerald earbobs. She did not know what the keys opened but they had always been in the box. Lily feared that as soon as she removed them, she would find a need for the odd keys. So she kept both odd keys. 'Twas a quirk of her mind but one she could not get over.

Standing before the looking glass earbobs in place, Lily straightened her shoulders. Her breasts rose to reveal a bit more than a modest amount of cleavage. Being a woman with a mind of her own, or so she prided herself, she faithfully ignored the current fashion of piling her flaming curls atop her head. The popular style only increased her height, which did not suit her at all. Instead, her maid Jane pulled Lily's auburn locks back and pinned them with tortoise combs, allowing a thick mass of loose curls to tumble past her shoulders.

Jane's voice held a bit of wonder. "I have never seen you look as beautiful."

"I must look as well as possible if I am to succeed."

"You cannot fail."

"Oh!" Lily started when the old corridor clock struck. Her da had ordered the Longcase Drumhead clock from Edinburgh's finest clockmaker, the young Robert Bryson. The drumhead had been his pride and joy. Unexpected tears gathered behind her eyes as she listened to the clock's familiar chime signaling the supper hour had arrived.

After one last check in the cheval mirror and a pinch of her cheeks to add a bit of color, she hurried from the refuge of the faded blue chamber. Her nerves very nearly screamed with excitement as she neared the first-floor dining hall and came ever closer to another encounter with Edan.

But as she neared instead of one male voice, she heard several.

A bubble of disappointment broke deep in her belly.

Admonishing herself for having no reason to feel disappointed, she paused at the entrance of the room—and peeked. Beneath the flickering light of crystal candelabras and wall sconces, three broad, tall men awaited her, and they seemed to be talking at once. In addition to Edan, Lily recognized his younger brothers, Angus and Finlay—whom everyone called Finn. Only Jamie and Donald were absent. Evidently, she would not be dining alone with Edan. Another heavy wave of disappointment swept through her. Disconcerting, all this disappointment.

The Cameron brothers were a striking, brawny group of men, the core of a clan unlike any others. She smiled as she gazed upon the three gathered at the table. There wasn't a woman in all of England or Scotland who wouldn't give her soul for the opportunity to be dining alone with the Cameron men. None, that is, but Lily. She had looked forward to charming one man. Nay, in truth she'd meant to seduce him. Instead, 'twas apparent she must charm each of his brothers into believing she would make the best wife for Edan. Lifting her chin, she sailed forward, hoping she was up to the task.

Lily cleared her throat to alert the brothers to her presence as she entered the dining hall. A sudden silence descended on the hall except for the scraping of chairs on stone. All eyes were upon her making her feel exceedingly uncomfortable. Each of the fine young men stood, welcoming her with warm smiles. Fixing what she supposed to be a brilliant smile to her lips, she nodded to each in turn.

Edan reigned at the head of the polished mahogany table, as rivetingly handsome as a man could possibly be. Even with his glower. For the briefest moment, the sight of him caused Lily to become breathless. Her smile to falter. The scar raging across his cheek spoke of courage in battle, the mark of a warrior and a man to be reckoned with and respected. He motioned for her to take the empty chair to his right and stood to hold it for her.

She bobbed a slight curtsy. "Good evening, gentlemen, 'tis lovely to see you again."

The brothers responded simultaneously booming greetings in their melodic Scottish burrs. Not a word was clear to her. Though they spoke English, Lily could not understand a single sentence. But the brothers' wide smiles and appreciative glances struck an unexpected wave of warmth that flowed through her from head to toe, making truth of her polite greeting.

She shifted her gaze to Edan's left where his ginger-bearded brother Angus sat. Lily recalled the fun-loving Angus as a boisterous man, a bit slovenly but loving, like a clumsy young lion cub. The next oldest to Edan, he would be quite good-looking if it weren't for his thick beard which made him appear quite fearsome. However, the twinkle in his light, bright blue eyes quickly dispelled the notion the big man might be a menace.

Finn, who most resembled Edan in his darkly attractive way, sat quietly next to Angus. She recalled Finlay Cameron as a man of few words, quiet and intelligent. He possessed gray-blue eyes, a gentle smile, and a calm disposition.

Edan raised his glass. "To Lilith Munro, we welcome ye back to Glen Carin."

"Slainte!" the brothers chorused as one.

Chapter 3

Finn smiled. "'Tis a pleasure to welcome ye home, Mistress Lilith."

"Aye, and ye must stay as long as ye like," Angus added with a wide bear-like grin.

Edan snorted.

Lilly beamed.

Although the chief of the clan had held her chair, Edan had not complimented Lily on her appearance. His gaze, however, had lingered in the area of her breasts for longer than seemly. The heat of a blush burned on her cheeks.

Except for the laird none of the brothers had dressed for supper. Although they knew she would be dining with them, Finn and Angus were obviously wearing the same clothing they'd worked in all day. A habit of long standing most likely, she thought. Scanning the haphazardly set table, Lily felt a long way from a Mayfair dinner party.

"As you can see, my brothers were eager to greet ye," Edan said, pausing to slant what appeared to be an after-the-fact smile.

"Thank you." She glanced from Finn to Angus with a nod. "I am so happy to see you. Your presence makes me feel more at home than ever."

"'Tis yer home as long as ye are a Munro," Finn said. Pausing, his gentle gaze rested on hers. "After

Edan purchased Glen Carin from Lady Frances, we brothers separated. Angus and I continue to live at Castle Cameron, while Jamie and Edan live here in Glen Carin."

"'Tis a comfortable arrangement?"

"Aye."

"Ah, Lilith, ye are more bonnie than we could have imagined," Angus told her. "The last time we saw ye, ye were—"

"A bit of a ruffian?" Edan interrupted.

Angus paled.

Lily laughed. "I understand. My rascal lass reputation has lingered. 'Tis true I was a bit of a...scamp. But I haven't climbed a tree in an exceedingly long time. Although, every once in a while, I confess I do feel the urge to do so."

"Do ye no' recall when ye leaped down upon me from a tree limb whilst I was breaking in my new mount?" Edan grumbled.

"An unfortunate accident," she assured him quickly. "Did I cause you pain?"

"Nay. Dinna be silly."

"Will yer sister be joining us?" Angus asked.

With a soft shake of her head and a sigh, Lily answered, "I fear the journey was too much for her. Charlotte is a fragile young woman. She will require extra rest."

Edan's stony gaze fixed on her.

Lily responded with a bright smile. She meant only to reassure him.

A procession of servants headed by Netta, the unsmiling housekeeper prevented further conversation. The young men and women served what Lily could only conclude to be a feast. One after another steaming dishes of barley broth, kale, mutton, Aberdeen beef, salmon, partridge, and tatties were placed on the table.

"Have you come for the ceilidh?" Finn asked when the servants left.

"A ceilidh?" Lily repeated, pronouncing the word correctly as kay-lee. Although she hadn't heard the Gaelic word in years; she remembered a ceilidh as being a festive gala that oftentimes grew out-of-hand, in a pleasant way. "You are holding a ceilidh here in Glen Carin?"

Edan waved a dismissive hand. "Nothing of consequence."

Finn with gray eyes alight, shot Lily a warm smile. "It's to be a celebration of our return to the Highlands."

"Aye," affirmed Angus. "'Twill be an offering of goodwill and hope to all of our Highland neighbors. Together we shall prosper again."

"What a grand idea! I adore a ceilidh!" She remembered the music, dancing and singing as a time of great joy, a respite from the hard life of the Highland farmers. Obviously, Edan's brothers did not consider the planned ceilidh to be of no consequence.

"Every mother and daughter from miles around will be invited," Angus boomed. He lowered his voice and added with a mischievous grin. "We are looking for wives, ye ken. We wish the help of good Highland women."

"All three of you?" Lily blurted in surprise. "You and Finn are looking for wives as well as Edan?"

The ever-practical brother, Finn explained, "'Tis time. The fighting between France and England has ended. We must restore what has been lost and build a new life on our land. We canna do it alone. We need partners."

"What sort of woman are you looking for, Finn?" she asked.

"A quiet lass, smart and able to work beside me whether it be in the fields or in the house." He paused for a moment then grinned, adding, "A lass who is bonnie would be vera nice."

"Of course. You deserve a bonnie lass." She smiled, turning to the big bear of the brothers, "Angus, what kind of woman would you like?"

"I dinna ken." He frowned in though, pulling at his beard. "A lass large and strong to match me. A lass able to bear many children."

"And would you like your helpmate to be a bonnie lass?" Lily pressed.

"Aye, but no bonnie lass has ever looked my way. A plain-lookin' lass will do. I'll know her when I see haer."

Lily turned to Edan. His taciturn features gave no indication of what he might be thinking as he cut into his mutton. Fearing to ask the laird what he wished for in a woman in case she might not like his answer, she asked another question. "When is your ceilidh to be held?"

Before he could reply, Finn answered, "In ten days' time."

"Ye are under no obligation to stay, Lilith," Edan interjected quickly, noting to his brothers, "Glen Carin lacks the comforts the *lady* is accustomed to."

Lily protested at once. "I would not miss your ceilidh for the world. And my sister! Charlotte will be so pleased. I shall send a message to my mother explaining our delay immediately."

"Let us not talk aboot ceilidh and wives," Edan declared, "when we can talk of sheep."

"Perhaps I can help you with the planning," she suggested. "Of the ceilidh."

Edan leaned toward her. His frown ran deep. "Eh?"

"I shall be happy to help plan the ceilidh. Have you made any of the arrangements? I should be delighted to make a list. You shall need musicians and—"

"Netta! More mutton," Edan called out.

"On the morrow I shall find a bell to call your servants," Lily said. Mindful of offending him, she offered the laird what she thought to be her sweetest smile. "So much…simpler than shouting."

Netta hurried in with more mutton. Goblets of ale were replenished before they were empty.

Conversation was kept to the minimum as the brothers wolfed down their meal. Lily was so nervous she could barely swallow. The brothers eyed her from time to time, taking her measure in obvious fashion. 'Twas unsettling. However, news of a ceilidh gave her a reason to remain at Glen Carin. She had come to the conclusion that winning Edan over to her marriage plan might take longer than she'd anticipated. It did not bode well that he had not readily accepted her proposal. Apparently, she had shocked him. Something she had not considered.

At one point during the meal, Angus paused between mouthfuls to assure her, "After we sup I'll play ye some tuns on my pipe."

"That would be lovely," she answered. Lilly hoped the eager-to-please man played the bagpipe better than she remembered. Back then he'd fancied himself a musician of the caliber of young Chopin. Angus, the Chopin of pipers.

She could bear sour notes here and there now that she'd earned a reprieve of time by volunteering to help with the ceilidh. Certainly, she could use the time to her advantage in the seduction of Edan. By providing a successful ceilidh, she would prove her worth to him as a partner, as well as keeping the other women vying for his hand at bay. Lily had no doubt Edan was deemed a valuable prize in the Highland marriage market.

While she sipped ale, she gazed about the dining hall. The furnishings were those appointed by Lady Frances years ago. Nothing had been changed or replaced. The furnishings, from the tapestries at either end of the room to the gold silk drapes to the once beautiful Aubusson carpet were the same, and all had grown shabby. Even so, the setting was similar to those found in the best of London society homes.

Her Scot father had built the spacious estate in the fashion of all great English manors especially for his beautiful English bride. Most tenants and townsfolk regarded the sprawling manor, set in the heather-strewn hillside, as the finest dwelling in the Highlands. But Lily's mother had disliked it all at first sight; the three-story red brick manor, the bone-chilling climate, the rugged country, and especially the hearty Highlanders she derided as barbarians—when she was being kind.

Lily had never felt the same as her mother. She'd loved her home in the Highlands. Memories flooded back to her without end. After so many years away, would her da be happy if he could see her now surrounded by Camerons in the great dining hall? She missed her father fervently. But here, here in the manor he'd built, she felt his presence and his love keenly. She was meant to be here. Lily knew it. Her feelings ran deep. Feelings that gave her courage. Courage she would need.

She glanced around the table. Although she'd always favored Edan, Lily admired the Cameron men. Each one of them. Good men, handsome men, even now when shoveling in their food as if they hadn't eaten in months. The manners of the Highlanders remained—well, Highlanders.

The four-course meal ended with raspberries and ale. Always more ale. Lily relaxed in a tide of relief, most certainly the result of the ale.

Steepling his huge hands, Edan leaned back in his chair, regarding Lily thoughtfully. Her gaze fixed on his hands wondering how… No! She must not consider for a moment how his touch would feel. She lifted her goblet once again and gulped.

"If we are to succeed competing in business with the English, and we shall, 'tis time for us to acquire the same drawing room manners, as well as profitable crops and herds," Edan said. His smile lacked warmth; resolve darkened his eyes.

After observing how the Camerons launched into their supper, she understood how a bit of polish might be in order.

"While my brothers and I were away fighting with Welllngton for the English King, our land went fallow and our herds grew scrawny, at least those remaining. Half our cattle were stolen. Just look about ye, Lilith, at how the manor has been sadly neglected."

She gave a slight nod before Edan responded with the answer Lily did not wish to hear. "This is why we search for hearty Highland lasses to take as our wives and working partners. Good lasses who will work beside us to restore our homes and land." Again, he emphasized. *hearty* and *Highland.*

"I see." Convinced she qualified at the very least as a Highland-born woman, Lily favored Edan with what she hoped her loveliest smile. Later, she would worry about proving her strength and learning just what he meant by *good lasses.*

"You do?" he asked with a wary lilt to his voice. "Ye understand?"

"Oh, yes. Aye." With each passing moment and each sip of ale, she became even more convinced, although he did not realize it yet; she would make the perfect wife for Edan. She'd arrived just in time to prevent him from making a lifelong mistake. 'Twould be a grievous mistake if the Highland lasses' gift of a laird married anyone but her.

"In order to prosper in our tenuous alliance with the British, we Highlanders must obtain the manners necessary to mingle as gentlemen in the clubs and drawing rooms with the English and Edinburgh ton as well. To that end, my brothers and I request yer guidance, Lilith," he paused and fixed his dark gaze upon her. "If ye stay to prepare our ceilidh."

Lily attempted to stifle her gasp of surprise, sucking in air that caused her to choke. Instruct the Camerons in drawing room manners in ten days? Lessons that would require at least a year or two? Impossible.

"Are ye all right?" Finn asked, leaning toward her, concern darkening his eyes.

"Would ye like me to play my pipes fer ye no'?"

Angus asked, jumping up from his chair.

"No, no," she protested. "I'm quite fine." Only she was not fine. What Edan asked was impossible! In so many ways. It would take quite a miracle for Angus Cameron alone to learn the proper manners which would enable him to appear in a proper ton drawing room. "I...I...would like to help of course," she said as soon as she recovered, "But, but—"

Edan interrupted, "Ye've spent most of your life in London. Who better to instruct us? Unless you canna stay..."

"I did not say nay," she responded swiftly. If she agreed to his proposition, would Edan accept her proposal? Were they bargaining? She could not ask with his brothers in attendance. Instead, Lily raised her goblet and downed half the ale before replying. "To be clear, you wish me to instruct the manners of the ton," she repeated in a raspy voice.

"Aye," Edan affirmed, tilting back in his chair, narrowing his gaze upon her. An enigmatic smile played on his lips. "While I possess some knowledge, Finn and Angus have little or none."

His lips. She focused on his lips. How at once in a rush of heat and unbidden desire she wished for his lips on hers. *Mother Have Mercy!* What was she thinking?

Biding her time, Lily took two unladylike swallows of ale and drained the goblet. After clearing her throat, she said, "And also plan a ceilidh?"

"Aye. 'Tis an honor ye requested."

She angled her head, deep in fuzzy thought.

"Do ye think us so dull we canna learn?" a scowling Angus asked. "Ye think no lass will have a Cameron no matter no'?"

"No!" At present, she was working on keeping her lightheaded thoughts straight. "Nay," she repeated quickly. "Not at all. I am simply not certain I see the need."

Netta stepped in and refilled Lily's empty goblet.

Edan's dark brows dove into a deep frown. "'Tis a need. Unlike my brothers, I have been fortunate to have spent a good deal of time in London. But even I would benefit by lessons from a lady. A *lady* like yourself."

Why did Edan keep emphasizing lady? 'Twas worrisome. *Did he not believe she was a lady?* "I, I shall do my best," she replied inhaling deeply.

"Have we struck a bargain then?"

"Indeed, we have." She hiccupped.

Edan's gaze met hers once more.

The heat of a roaring fire flooded through her body.

"My brothers and I will expect a lesson from ye every evening at supper."

"Ooh."

"And of course, the Cameron ceilidh must be the largest and finest of any gathering seen for miles around."

Of course.

"Ten days," she murmured. "I shall call upon the Doonies to help me."

Edan dipped his head, a wry smile on his lips. "Are ye speaking of the Doonies who come to us in our dreams?"

"They live here in Glen Carin."

"Aye?"

She leaned forward to whisper, "My da told me so."

"Then it must be so," he declared with a chuckle. "Lilith, I challenge you to transform the Cameron brothers from farmers to gentlemen. And to present a ceilidh no Highland lad or lassie will ever forget."

Lily's head spun. She had never taught manners nor planned a ceilidh—which did not mean she could not. She lifted her goblet again in salute. "I accept your challenge."

The ale seemed to calm her nerves.

At last the meal ended. Lily relaxed, observing the brothers as they sat back appearing satisfied. Somehow even in weariness the Camerons exuded a sense of comfort in home and family.

Edan gestured for the goblets to be refilled once more before he turned to Lily. "'Tis important you understand, Lilith. Now that the war with France is finished and Napoleon banished, there is no longer any doubt," he began. "The English have prevailed, thanks to the bravery of the Highlanders in our 42nd Highland Regiment."

"The Black Watch," Lily said softly, demonstrating her knowledge of Scotland's esteemed fighters to the brothers. She took pride in her Scot's blood. And she felt it important that the Cameron brothers know.

"The British have also secured Scotland as well," he continued, frowning. Meeting her gaze he continued in a softer voice, laced with bitterness, "We have become one nation again with Great Britain."

Lowering her eyes, she shifted uncomfortably in her chair. *Did Edan hold her English mother against her?*

There were grunts about the table. Clearly, this fact did not make any of the proud Cameron men happy.

Lily could well understand the men's feelings but was unable to think of anything to say that might ease their anguish.

"We have been more fortunate than most," Edan went on.

"Aye," said Finn. "For Edan's bravery and exemplary service to the crown during the Battle of Waterloo, King George gifted him with…with our own land, land that had been the Cameron land for decades."

"And a title," Angus added. "Did ye ken Edan is now the Viscount of Bennington?"

"Noooo…"

"As well as the Laird of Glen Carin and chief of the Cameron Clan," Finn added with undisguised pride.

"I did not know," she said, her surprise tempered by the ale and exhaustion creeping over her. "What a great honor. Edan, you have done well. I am proud to know you." *What was she saying? Was that what she meant to say?*

"My brothers fought by my side," Edan said. "And while we fought, our farm, the fields and the herds fell to ruin."

Finn nodded, continuing the Cameron's story. "We left Donald in charge and dinna ken he had been killed by rogues until we hastened back—to the ruins."

"We are still in the early stages of restoration," Edan added.

"Aye, but we have made great progress," Finn cut in. "We are Highlanders, and we shall not be defeated." His quiet but impassioned statement reminded Lily of the Highlanders' unerring pride. "'Tis good to have a bonnie Highland lass at our table," he added. "One who can teach us the manners and the way of speaking like the educated English ton."

"Bonnie and tall," Angus put in. "Ye are tall, Lily," he remarked idly, as if she did not know.

She nodded, first toward Finn and then to Angus. With every movement her head grew lighter and spun. Confusion claimed her. "Thank you," she answered, for lack of anything coming to mind. *Anything!*

A searing heat settled on Lily's cheeks. Disturbing her. Simple dinner conversation had never eluded her before. Or was it Edan's nearness?

During the meal, the long, long meal, every move the laird made had seemed to warm her. While she had anticipated there would be problems during her journey, she had not expected this sort of problem. Her attraction to the dark-haired, lusty Highlander threatened her in ways she dared not contemplate. She'd come to marry him, not to lose her heart to the compelling laird.

For a few moments she felt as if she and Edan were alone in the hall. His gaze fixed on her, on her alone. She'd been focused solely on him, on his eyes, his mouth, and his broad shoulders. Lily had almost forgotten that Angus and Finn lingered and listened.

She took a deep breath. And then another. Dizzy, with head swimming, she reached for her goblet. Her hands shook. She feared she might be sick at any moment.

"I believe I require air. Fresh air."

"Nay, Lily. The garden is vera dark. I shall play me pipe."

Edan shook his head in warning. "Nay, Angus."

Netta and her kitchen servants hoovered like ghosts, quietly slipping empty plates and bowls from the table. Candles spluttered and light died like fireflies giving flight and vanishing into the night.

****

Edan, the Laird of Glen Carin, Viscount of Bennington, and Chieftain of the Cameron Clan watched Lilith closely. He was confident on the morrow when she realized she had been given responsibility of a successful ceilidh and making over his brothers into ton worthy gentlemen, she would call off her proposal and hasten back to London as quickly as possible. Until then, he meant to avoid further conversation and any more time alone in her company than necessary. The presence of his brothers he deemed necessary, for there was safety in numbers.

But should he worry about the vacant look in the beauty's eyes? When first she'd entered the dining room, her large spring-bright eyes had shined with an eager light when her gaze met his. She'd appeared happy to see him. Her smile made him feel a wee bit uncomfortable since he found her presence to cause the pit of his stomach to drop in a most unpleasant manner. Just as it had in years past. When, then as now, he could not guess what new mischief lay in the back of the mettlesome lass's mind, and he feared the worst.

Dismissing his apprehension, Edan decided it must be the ale that had dulled Lilith's gaze. Most likely she hadn't enjoyed one of Scotland's favorite beverages for some time. In the heavy silence, he studied her surreptitiously. When she looked from Angus to Finn, Lilith's curls, the color of a deep scarlet sunset, swept her shoulders in an enticing manner. He felt an unexpected and quite unnerving longing to reach out and grasp a handful of her thick, shining locks.

Seeking respite from untoward feelings, he lowered

his eyes. And stopped. His gaze lingered on the low cut of her gown and the pale porcelain cleavage that ignited a swift and sure heat within him. Like a wind-whipped wildfire, a sudden hot surge of lust flowed through his veins. Damn!

At that unanticipated moment, the beautiful brat reached out, rested a hand on his arm and raised a wide, pleading gaze to his. And then came the coup d'état. She batted her lashes at him. Those long entrancing lashes. His heart raced like a hound in hunt.

"I wish to learn the waltz," Angus said. "They say 'tis all the rage in London."

"Yes, 'tis," she murmured.

Edan thought it a lopsided smile Lilith had given his brother. He'd never seen her give a lopsided smile before, although it was a wee bit entrancing. Was she up to mischief? She might require a closer watch.

"We should learn how to dress in proper ton fashion as well," Finn put in, shifting his gaze pointedly toward Angus's dirty shirt.

"Jamie 'ill return from London soon. He'll 'elp ye…" Did she say, ye? She meant you. "…with trews and su-such," Lilith assured them, slurring her words slightly.

"Jamie has a bit of the devil in him. We canna rely on his ability to instruct us in the proper English ways," Finn noted.

Edan leaned forward toward Lilith. "We dinna intend to be Englishmen. We are Highlanders and proud to be. But like it or not, change is upon us, and we must flow with the even' tide. We canna be regarded as the savage Scot outsiders and hope for success."

"I understand," she said, pausing, regarding the amber ale in her goblet as she swirled the liquid. "I do, I undershand but—" her voice trailed off. She appeared mesmerized by the liquid in motion.

Edan rested a gentle hand on her arm. Her flesh beneath his hand was warm and soft as silk to his touch. It took a mighty effort to resist the urge to stroke her arm. Guilt pricked under his skin for pressuring her. But the sooner Lilith understood she had landed in over her depth, the better. The safer he would feel. "Will you help us, Lilith?"

Her long dark lashes fluttered with nervousness or agitation, he could not know which, but he felt her resistance melting.

"For auld time's sake," he added softly.

"Aye, is the only answer a Cameron accepts," boomed Angus.

She gazed at each of Edan's brothers for a long moment before raising her great jeweled eyes to Edan's. "Aye," she replied in barely a whisper. "We shall begin dance leshons to, to prepare for the ceilidh."

Edan raised his goblet in salute, "To Lilith!"

His brothers followed his lead and the dining room echoed with her name, "To Lilith!"

Her slight smile wavered for only a moment before she too lifted her goblet and proceeded to quaff the rest of the pale amber liquid.

Concern gnawed at Edan. He'd lain on the pressure as thick as day old porridge. A wee bit of guilt made its way into the emotional mix. His childhood tormenter looked pale. She'd gone as white as the snow-capped mountains of Skye. Her eyes were blank.

"I feel, I feel a bit faint," she whispered.

"A wee dram of Scotch whiskey will put ye to rights again," Angus told her. "Or a wee tun on me pipes."

Lilith gave him a weak smile. Giving a little shake of her head she said, "I fear I am quite exhausted." She turned to Edan. "Please excuse me, I mush retire now."

Splaying her hands on the table, with what looked to be a forced and definitely feeble smile, she stood, wavered, wobbled—and sank.

Edan caught her before she hit the floor.

Angus and Finn groaned in almost simultaneous harmony.

Lilith Munro had passed out.

Chapter 4

Silencing his brothers with a sharp glance, Edan swept Lilith into his arms and carried the sleeping beauty up the stairs and down the long corridor to her bedchamber. She weighed little more than a sack of seed and smelled faintly of roses, a soothing, feminine scent. Moaning softly, she snuggled against his chest. His heart leapt like the heart of a young buck. It was all he could do not to kiss her sweet lips, lips beckoning him to taste her.

Edan growled in frustration. The last thing he wanted was this unexpected feeling of desire for Lilith, the devil-child of his youth. He would give all the heather in Scotland for her to be gone, to be out of his life once again.

Kicking her chamber door open, he strode past her astonished maid. Easing his guest's limp body down on the bed, he barked at her wide-eyed maid. "Take care of Lady Lilith. She may feel sickly on the morrow."

Reminding himself that he was a Highlander raised to fight with the blade, musket, and at last resort an iron fist, Edan tromped out of Lilith's chamber. He refused to weaken, to allow her entry into his well-planned life. Or to his heart. As the first-born son of a ruthless warrior, he'd learned his lessons well at the hands of his father. Any misdeed, no matter how large or small on Edan's part would meet with a savage beating from his da. 'Twas Edan's misfortune to serve as an example to his younger brothers for any offense, perceived or not.

He watched as his father berated his mother on every occasion. Despite loving him and bearing her husband five healthy sons, she served as the object of his scorn. Edan suffered for his obedient mother. Her love had not protected her and in the end, she had died of a broken heart.

His da had not known how to love—and had not taught Edan to love.

Edan had given little thought to love in his life. He'd seen the unhappy results of love, the pain and grief love had brought to his mother. He refused to torment any woman in such a manner. Even Lilith. Secretly, Edan worried that he might have inherited his Da's darkness. He feared the same black heart would someday surface in him. An arranged marriage suited him, with a woman who did not expect his love. His requirement was simple: a partner to work beside him and to give him an heir. A partner he would keep at a distance.

A sixth sense told him this would not be Lilith Munro. The Scot in her would not settle for anything less than his complete attention. No matter what she said about the joy of an arranged marriage, Lilith would demand his love. Something he did not have and so could not give her.

Edan's and therefore his clan's well-being, depended upon his focus, as well as on his physical strength, emotional detachment, and intelligence. Listening to the heart brought death and disaster.

Edan made decisions based on facts. He needed a woman but not a mischief maker who caused his heart to skip. But how to convey his message without causing tears stumped him. Nothing he'd said during supper seemed to daunt Lilith. She had agreed to plan the ceilidh, only ten days away, and teach his brothers all they would need to know in order to make an impression with their future British colleagues. The bold lass would soon realize she did not possess the makings of a strong Highlands woman. 'Twas one thing to boast of skills and another to actually possess them. Lilith had been pampered in English comfort most of her life. She'd become soft and unfit for Highland life. He would prove it.

****

"Oooh. Oooh." Moaning did not relieve the throbbing headache and unsettled stomach Lily woke with the next morning. With each chime of the Longcase clock, her head reverberated with pain. She could not even count the hours struck. She'd sipped more of the bitter tasting amber liquid until she'd done the most humiliating thing imaginable—and passed out.

"Jane!"

Her maid ran from the small adjoining servant's chamber. "Yes, milady."

"What is the time?"

"'Tis almost noon."

"Oh, no. What of Charlotte?"

"She is fine. She broke fast in her chamber and awaits you."

"Oh no."

This journey had not gotten off to a propitious start. Her sister was sick and scared, and oh dear, after last night, what must Edan think of Lily now? She had attempted to soothe her extremely frayed nerves with ale at dinner and had passed out in so doing. Had she ruined her chances to make a marriage arrangement? Lily refused to think it! She would recover Edan's respect by arranging the finest ceilidh the Highlands had ever experienced. She would win the handsome laird's esteem, if not his love.

"Help me, Jane. I must get dressed. There's no time to waste."

From this day forth, Lily resolved to keep her mission uppermost in her mind. She had returned to marry Edan; she had not come back to win the magnificent laird's heart or to fall in love with him all over again. She was no longer a child. Still, with the first look at her old friend, her heart had caught fire. But she must not give way to any distraction. Charlotte's future was at stake.

Lily had no time for regrets or the luxury of lingering in bed. She meant to impress Edan with a grand ceilidh, although she had never actually planned such a festive event.

Her mother had brought Lily to this mortifying state. If it were not for Lady Frances's spendthrift ways, a hasty forbidden marriage for Charlotte would not be necessary. Ah, but there seemed to be no help for Lady Frances. The woman had been married three times and been widowed three times.

At this point, no man in Great Britain would consider marrying Lady Frances unless he secretly harbored a death wish. Unless an unenlightened gentleman quite suddenly appeared, Lily's mother appeared doomed to remain a widow for life. Worse, in Lily's opinion, was that her mother had never really loved any of her husbands.

Desperate, and quite unable to curb her reckless spending, Lady Frances turned to her daughters to support her in her dotage. She schemed to marry Lily and Charlotte into wealth and grand titles. Much to Lily's chagrin, Lady Frances possessed the connections to do so.

Lollygagging in her chamber served no purpose with so much to accomplish if progress was to be made. Her head still throbbed when she left her bedchamber and knocked softly on Charlotte's door.

The door opened slowly. Charlotte's hair had not been brushed and she still wore her wrinkled white linen night shirt and dressing gown.

"Sweet, how are you feeling this morn?"

She sighed. A much-maligned sigh. "I feel like a prisoner. I cannot leave this chamber by myself. So I wait for you. Always wait for you. You promised to protect me."

"You are safe anywhere in Glen Carin, in the garden, or any chamber. You do not have to remain secreted away and you do not have to wait for me."

"I am beginning to understand Mama's dislike of Glen Carin."

"Mama would not be happy anywhere. If you remember, almost as soon as she left Glen Carin, she discarded her mourning garments and married the Marquis of Dillingham."

"I remember. They were only married six months when the marquis fell off his horse during a hunt and broke his neck. Poor Mama."

"No, poor Mama. If you recall, following a barely suitable period of mourning for Dillingham, she remarried Viscount Rothsfield. That union lasted a mere three years before the viscount met his end, struck down by apoplexy."

Charlotte nodded. "I liked Rothsfield."

"Unfortunately, he did not prove to be as affluent as Mama had been led to believe. Our mother's love of fine food, Paris fashion and gambling has brought her to the brink of financial disaster."

Ever resourceful, with no new husband in sight, Lady Frances schemed. She chose Charlotte, her youngest, prettiest, and most biddable daughter to marry off first.

"Which is why we are in hiding at Glen Carin," Charlotte sighed.

"We are not hiding, sweet. We are making new arrangements."

Lily could not allow her eighteen-year-old sister to be married to a man three times her age, who suffered from gout, wickedly bad breath, and a tendency to beat his wives, according to the gossips. Lady Frances's assurances that the whispered rumors surrounding the death of Whetfield's last wife were just that, horrid rumors, did not ease Lily's mind.

Charlotte sank to her bed. "Has the laird accepted your proposal?"

"Not yet. But he will. 'Tis too soon."

"I feel the start of another headache."

"Sweet, we have been invited to remain for a gala in less than ten days. I promise you the best time with music, bagpipes, and fiddles. We'll dance and feast on platters brimming over with fresh salmon, scones, and shortbread, and anything you'd like."

"I'd like?"

"Yes."

Charlotte slanted a questioning gaze. "Who will come to this gala?"

"Highlanders from miles around. And, well, since we are planning the gala, it will—"

Charlotte's lovely forehead wrinkled in a formidable frown. "We? You and I are planning the gala? Is it customary for the guests to plan the galas in Scotland?"

Lily shrugged. "I do not think of us as guests. Glen Carin is our home."

The creases in Charlotte's forehead grew deeper. "Must I leave my bedchamber to plan?"

"Although I do not understand your reluctance to leave, the answer is no. Not at first."

Giving a firm nod, Charlotte stood. "All right then, I'll help. Perhaps Jamie will be back in time for the gala."

"Jamie?"

"Perhaps," Charlotte shrugged.

A blush of pink colored her cheeks, belying Charlotte's nonchalance regarding Jamie. But Lily had no time at present for the questions tumbling through her mind. "Yes, sweet. Jamie may indeed return in time for the ceilidh."

Charlotte lowered her head.

"I will share supper here with you this eve." Having secured a truce of sorts with her petulant sister, Lily slowly made her way to the morning room.

Platters of breakfast foods were lined along the buffet. Much to her dismay, the strong aromas of sausage, porridge and kippers filled the room. Her stomach lurched. She pressed a hand against her middle.

Grateful to find herself alone, Lily poured a cup of tea, took a sip, and placed it on the table. 'Twas then her tortoise hair comb came loose. She went down on her knees to poke her head beneath the heavy furniture and found it. While there, she thought to look for the Doonie Purse which might have fallen behind the buffet. Who knew?

"Lilith?"

Edan's voice gave her such a start, her entire body jerked, and she banged her aching head on the bottom of the buffet. She'd been so intent on her quest she hadn't heard him coming. Slowly easing her body from beneath the heavy piece of furniture, she rubbed the fresh knot atop her throbbing head.

"Are ye all right?" he asked, extending a hand to help her up.

No!

"Yes." She smiled up at him.

"I confess I do not often find my guests on the floor."

"Aye. But then…But then I am not an ordinary guest."

"Quite true."

For Edan to discover her on hands and knees with her derriere in the air did not bode well. She forced a wide smile and soothed the muslin skirt of her pale blue morning dress as if nothing were amiss and her explanation completely understandable.

He arched one dark, inquiring brow. "Dare I ask what ye were doing on the floor beneath the buffet?"

"I, I heard something drop." She held up the hair comb in her hand. "'Twas my comb slipped out and rolled under the buffet."

He nodded. His heart-stopping deep-blue gaze settled on the strands of hair which had come undone. He reached out and tucked the fly-away strands behind her ear.

"Th-thank you." She splayed a hand over her ear, over the strands Edan had touched. She felt quite flushed. "I shall need to repair my…my hair."

"Immediately?"

"Oh. No. No." *Now that they were alone, had he decided to accept her proposal?*

Swallowing eagerness she could not deny, Lily took the moment to delight in the buzz of anticipation surging through her body. Strangely, her head had begun to clear at the first sight of Edan.

He shot her a puzzled frown as he held a chair for her.

Not the look Lily expected from a man about to accept her proposal. Her buzz fell flat. "I'm…I guess I am feeling a trifle unwell this morning," she confessed, as if that would explain her confusion.

"Our Scot whiskey and ale are vera strong beverages," he said, with a twist of his lips that may have been a suppressed smile.

She lowered her gaze. "Yes. Aye."

"Perhaps you imbibed a bit too much last eve."

"Undoubtedly. 'Twas the excitement of being back in Glen Carin."

One corner of his mouth curved up in return. "I dinna expect to see ye up and aboot this early, but 'tis well we can break fast together before I leave."

Oh, no! He could not wait to remove himself from her company!

"Leave? Where are you going?"

"To Cameron Castle."

"May I ride with you? I would very much like to see Cameron Castle again."

"I fear you could not keep up with me. 'Tis not a ride in Hyde Park I'll be making."

"You know I can keep up with you. I've not forgotten how to ride a horse, nor race. Do you not remember how we raced?"

"Aye. I do." Frowning, he darkly regarded the haggis on his plate.

"'Twould be delightful to see the countryside again as well," she said in her softest, most persuasive voice. "I promise not to slow your journey, nor interfere with your business at Cameron Castle."

"I do not ride with others, unless they are my brothers."

"You have ridden with me."

"Long ago." He raised his gaze to meet hers.

"I promise, Edan. Let me ride with you this morning and I shall not ask again."

"You promise?"

"I do."

"Well…"

"I'll change and meet you in the stables before you can mount your horse."

She was gone before he could stop her. Mumbling he'd been bested, Edan made his way to the stables.

The chill in the air was tempered by the heat from the sun as it slipped out from the clouds to shine on the pastures and over the meadows adjoining Glen Carin.

****

Edan prepared to mount Dragon when he heard Lilith calling to him. Smiling broadly, she rushed toward the stables where he waited. He waited, impatiently and rightfully angry with himself for agreeing to allow the hellion to ride along with him. But perhaps a rugged ride through the country would persuade her that the Highland life would no longer suit her.

Dressed warmly in a forest green pelisse and wearing boots, she arrived out of breath.

"This is your horse," he said, holding the reins out to her. "Bonnie is her name."

"She is a bonnie mare," Lilith exclaimed, taking the reins. "Indeed."

"She may be a bit high strung as she hasn't been ridden in a while."

"Do not ye fash," she said, flashing a smile with the use of the Scot word *fash* for worry. "Bonnie and I will do just fine."

Edan doubted it but only grunted in reply. "Malcolm, my stableman will help you mount."

She flashed another winning smile this time directed at Malcolm which put the young man to the blush. Edan shook his head. Lilith's happy smile was disarming. "Let's be off."

He urged his mount forward and walked the horse out of the stable yards and into the path. Ever so slowly as they left the immediate grounds of Glen Carin, he pushed Dragon into a canter.

"Faster!" Lilith cried from behind him.

He refused to disappoint. One reckless ride might send her back to London without him ever having to say nay to her proposal. As soon as they reached the open meadow, he gave Dragon his lead. Edan hadn't raced like this in many months, and to his surprise the wind against his face and the speed of the ride invigorated him. He felt like a young man again. Before long, Edan lost himself in the delight of the ride—until hearing the thunder of hooves beating beside him. Lilith!

He glanced to his right. She rode beside him, her reddened face alight with joy. Joy—there was no other word for what he saw. Edan had never seen her so glowing. He'd given her a sometimes problematic mare and a rugged ride—and unintentionally, he'd given her happiness. Strangely, as Lilith's pleasure bubbled over into laughter, a lighthearted feeling too long absent from his life swept through him.

Before long she surged ahead. The pins holding her hair fell and soon her thick mass of sunset curls flowed wild and free in the wind. Edan had never seen Lilith look so beautiful. His breath caught in his throat. There it was again! The wildness in her. The breath-taking wildness of Lilith.

Pulling on Dragon's reins, the big gelding slowed and Edan shouted. "Lilith!" He called her name several times before she heard him and slowed. She turned Bonnie back to where he waited.

Out of breath, eyes shining, she gasped her question, "Is something amiss, Edan?"

"Nay. Nothing. Nothing." Indeed, something felt amiss, but he could not say exactly what. "We're close to Cameron Castle and 'tis time to slow our pace."

Grinning, she nodded willingly. "But perhaps we can race on the way back to Glen Carin."

The twinkle in her eyes caused his heart to warm, to swell in a strange way. "Perhaps."

Minutes later they rode through the Cameron

Castle gates and were soon greeted by Finn. Lilith hovered near Edan as he discussed an addition to the castle with Finn. He'd planned to finish the restoration of Cameron Castle before starting on Glen Carin.

"The castle will be a lovely fortress once again," Lilith told Finn as she and Edan prepared to leave.

"I hope ye shall be our first visitor."

She replied to Finn's invitation with a smile and sprightly curtsey. "I never turn down an invitation to tea."

Once on their horses, Lilith rode sedately at Edan's side until out of sight of Cameron Castle. Before he could challenge her, she raced ahead, crying, "Catch me if you can!"

As many times as he'd been to Cameron Castle to discuss their plans with Finn, he'd not enjoyed himself half as much. The races, which he'd won, and the company of a woman free-spirited and smart had made a mundane task almost a pleasure.

"Thank you, Edan. 'Twas a fine morning."

"Aye," he agreed, when they'd returned to Glen Carin and reached the foyer. "I look forward to this eve." 'Twas the truth, he realized. He did look forward to being with Lilith again, though he should not. Closeness could pose a danger for her…and for him.

"I shan't be joining you this eve. Poor Charlotte has spent so much time alone; I must provide company for her. And it shall be time well spent, I promise you, for we shall begin planning the ceilidh."

Disappointment flowed through him like a bitter cold brew. And not at all to his liking. Lest she know how he truly felt, Edan nodded his understanding. 'Twas all he could do. He stalked away to his study.

The laird's steps echoed in the corridor as Lily looked after him. Her gaze lingered on the square set of his shoulders and his purposeful strides. She smiled, marveling at what a striking figure Edan posed—even while walking away.

Hours later, after bathing and resting, Lily retreated to Charlotte's chamber where they shared an early supper.

"Did the laird accept your proposal today?" Charlotte asked eagerly.

"Not yet."

Her sister's shoulders slumped. "But did you not spend a good deal of time with him today?"

"Aye. And I think he is coming around. Surely by the time Jamie returns, he will have proposed."

Her beautiful sister simply closed her eyes and shook her head, clearly shaking off any further discussion of Jamie. "*I* believe we should start work on your contingency plan, Lily."

"Edan has asked me to break fast with him in the morning and tell him the plans we have made for the gala."

"What plans?"

"The plans we shall make right now."

Lily gave Charlotte a confident smile. But secretly she feared her sister might be right. Edan had given her no indication he'd enjoyed spending the day with her. He'd spent hours with her but never mentioned marriage. At the very least, she'd hoped he might compliment her on retaining her riding skill, if he could not find anything else in her to admire.

Her search for the Doonie Purse must begin in earnest first thing on the morrow.

Chapter 5

Carrying her sketch pad and charcoals, Lily made her way to break fast, hoping she would find Edan. She was not disappointed.

The laird, looking more handsome than he had the day before, sat at the table wolfing down a sizable meal of haggis, eggs, tatties, and tea.

She greeted him brightly, "Good morn."

"Aye. 'Tis." After a brief regard and curt nod, he turned his attention to his eggs.

"Charlotte and I have made grand plans for your ceilidh. This morning I will speak with Netta about the help we shall need."

Again, another brisk nod before he rested his fork. "What is that?" he asked, bluntly pointing to Lily's sketch pad.

"'Tis my sketch pad where I sketch birds. I saw a Red Kite while we were out yesterday and hoped I might see him today."

"A kite?"

"A beautiful bird but most are gone from London."

"You sketch birds?"

She smiled broadly. At last he was discovering she was not just a drawing room needlepoint lady. A talent she possessed that perhaps he might admire.

But no.

He regarded her as if she might be slightly mad.

"Why? Why do ye sketch birds?"

"Because sketching brings me pleasure, and birds are such funny creatures. If they are disturbed, they can just fly away, as I have longed to do now and again," she admitted with a sigh.

"Sketching birds," he muttered, as if he'd never heard anything as strange. Pushing his plate aside he rose. "I must take my leave now, but I shall depart knowing all ceilidh planning is underway and under yer control."

"Can you not stay for a moment and hear our plans for the gala?"

"The ceilidh is woman's work. Ye dinna need me."

"But your approval is important."

"Nay, do whatever ye wish."

She dipped her head in a gesture of understanding. Understanding she would always offer Edan. Soon he would realize what a biddable woman she had become. Lily refused to allow him to see the disappointment in her eyes. But how was she to win his heart if he kept leaving her? She released another, deeper sigh. From this moment on, despite her growing anxiety she resigned to be all smiles and sweetness.

She lifted her gaze. He regarded her intensely, his gaze a smoky blue gray.

He took her breath away.

No! Lily would not allow Edan's amazingly broad shoulders or the perfectly symmetrical planes of his sun-darkened face to distract her from her mission. He must agree to their marriage within days—and she must resist the urge to run her finger lightly against the scar slashed across his cheek.

She shook off her wandering thoughts as he headed

toward the door. "Edan, I do not wish to interfere with your plans, but I would ask you to consider that neither of us are the same as when last we met. I believe we should spend time together and learn to know each other anew." She rushed on, not daring to take a breath in her effort to convince him of the rightness of wedding her. "We are older and wiser. We've had different experiences which have molded our minds apart from the young people we were years ago."

He swept a hand through his midnight hair. "I am a farmer now. My life is restoring Glen Carin and Cameron Castle. There is naught to interest ye."

"You went to war. You fought Napoleon. You were hurt. I would like to know about your experiences."

"On the battlefield? I'll tell ye no'. I ken how the English fight—like little lasses, most of them. But like my brothers, I ken little of how the English behave in their parlors. The Cameron clan needs to learn how the ton dresses for a ball and what a duke discusses with his dance partners at a ceilidh. 'Tis all I ask of ye, Lilith."

"You know I shall be honored and happy to help you."

"This may surprise ye," pausing, he threw her a caustic smile, "but during my brief time in London, I never received an invitation to Almacks."

Lily laughed. "Somehow, I cannot picture you in a top hat or engaging in small talk with Lady Jersey while drinking fruit punch at Almacks."

"I shall do what I must even if it should involve fruit punch."

"Tell me more, more of your life these past few years."

Biting his lower lip as if he was much pressed to give her an answer, Edan stared into space for several moments. He appeared torn between leaving and staying.

She remembered him as a young man when he had been as much of a devil as his younger brother Jamie. But Edan was no longer the young boy with the ready smile she remembered, the one she'd adored. Time and trouble, war and loss had taken its toll on the once wild young Highlander. He'd become his father's son, trapped in cold and darkness. She saw quite plainly sadness dwelled like a wary sentry in the laird's remarkable eyes.

"Are ye listening, Lilith?"

"Aye." *No!* Lost in her own thoughts, she'd heard not a word.

"My life at present is wholly devoted to restoring Castle Cameron and Glen Carin. If I had the funds, I would put matters to right immediately," Edan told her. "As 'tis, I'm selling our cattle one pasture at a time and purchasing the sheep which promise to be more profitable. The world is changing, and my clan must change as well."

The hard truth of the misfortune caused by the English; that had befallen the Cameron brothers left her without words.

"Lilith, yer return to the Highlands in our time of need is a fortunate happenstance." He stood, prepared to leave. "I welcome yer help learning English manners and with the ceilidh."

She nodded. She would have no answer to her proposal this morning. Her heart sank. "I shall do my best."

His gaze met hers before drifting to her lips. She swallowed hard as his mouth turned up in a half smile. Ripples of warmth washed down her spine.

The truth struck Lily with a start. Just the twist of Edan's rather sensuous lips could distract her from her quest. Under no circumstances must she let that happen again. She took a deep breath and added his lips to her list of possible distractions. Distractions she must resist.

"Dinna roam with yer birds. Stay close to the manor when ye sketch. Raiders have been seen in the area." A stern glance accompanied his warning.

"Will I see you at supper?"

He stalked off, calling over his shoulder, "Aye. I would no miss my first dance lesson."

Lily's heart jumped with renewed hope. Tonight she would teach a dance lesson and reveal her plans for the ceilidh. Edan would then agree to marry her without further procrastination. He would understand how much he needed her. Under no circumstances must she lose heart. She could not give up; 'twas too early in her quest to capture the laird's consent. Tonight everything would change.

****

Glen Carin's housekeeper greeted Lily with a scowl when she approached Netta in the kitchen a few minutes later. "Netta, I would like your help to plan a ceilidh."

Netta grunted and ambled away shaking her head. But she never ambled too far away. "Nay."

Lily followed. "I need help. I do not know who should be invited and how to arrange for music and food."

Without looking at Lily, the housekeeper floured

her hands and dug them into a ball of dough. "Ask me daughter Maisie to help."

"Might she come by this afternoon?"

"Tomorrow, if ye promise a wee bit of coin."

An unwanted delay, but nonetheless. "Fine. I will expect Maisie on the morrow for more than a wee bit of coin." *Lily would give the girl all the coin that she had left.*

With little else to be done about the ceilidh at present, Lily made her way to Charlotte's chamber. "Sweet, would you like to walk with me?"

"There is no sun."

If they were to wait for Highland sun, there might never be a walk.

"Charlotte, I miss your company."

"Has the laird accepted your proposal?"

"Nothing has changed since you asked me last. But it will." *She might pray on it.*

Rolling her eyes, Charlotte released an impatient sigh. "Your confidence is astonishing. But do not worry over me. Take your walk, I have my book," she held up the popular *Pride and Prejudice.* "And I wish to keep reading."

"All right then. I shall be off to sketch as I started to do this morn." But before she set out, she decided to start her search for the Doonie Purse. With Edan gone and Charlotte lost deep in the pages of a book, there seemed no better time.

She launched anew into her search, beginning with the ground floor rooms and occasionally running into Netta. Glen Carin's housekeeper greeted her with a suspicious eye each time. "Canna help?"

And each time Lily would reply with a bright

smile, "Nay. I am just reacquainting myself with the home of my youth."

Without fail, Netta grunted and ambled away shaking her head. But she never ambled too far from Lily.

Lily assumed the Doonie Purse to be small, almost fairy-sized. Although she didn't believe in fairies, she had no doubt the purse existed. Her da would not have told her of its existence and hinted at the purse's ability to help her in times of trouble if it did not.

Rob Munro read copiously, wrote wisely, and possessed a good and generous heart, a heart as large as Loch Ness. Unfortunately, his kindness was often mistaken for weakness or lack of intelligence. Lily knew differently.

Chafing under Netta's eagle eye and feeling excessively frustrated, she concluded a pause in her search would benefit her peace of mind until she could begin again.

****

Edan met Angus at the stables. Each day they rode to Cameron Castle by way of the pastures to make certain the sheep had not been stolen or killed by the Brodie clan. They also made a count of the cattle left to sell, a number rapidly diminishing.

Angus greeted him with a scowl. "Yer late."

"Lilith kept me. She chatters, ye know."

"Aye."

"She's up to some mischief."

"Aye? How dinna ken?"

"She told me she would be sketching birds."

"Birds, eh? She was always a wee bit of an odd lass. But why would ye think she's up to no good?"

"Because that is who Lilith is. She is a mischief-maker. She is no' one for watching birds nor sketching them."

"Ye speak of how ye knew her years ago. The lass may have changed."

"I don't trust her." *How could he? Young ladies of the ton played pianoforte and did needlepoint, they did not sketch birds.*

"She wants to marry ye and she's a bonnie lass. Ye don't need to trust her."

"Aye, I do."

He swung a big wide grin at Edan. "I'll marry her fer ye."

"Ye canna handle her. Let's go, Finn's waiting." Edan spurred Dragon. Riding, he could straighten his thoughts without Angus interfering.

He was a farmer. Lilith did not truly ken that was who he was now, what he'd always wanted to be against his father's wishes. His father had raised him to be a warrior when all he'd ever wanted to do was work the land and raise sheep. Now was the time he could make his dreams come true without worrying about his da. Edan's mind was set on repairing and putting to rights what the English had destroyed. And yes, he must marry. And with each new day that passed, it seemed he increasingly resisted the thought, the ease of marrying Lilith. Fearing he might bring the bird-loving beauty the pain he'd seen his mother suffer prevented him from surrendering. Lilith might be a bit mad, but she did not deserve to be treated ill.

Thoughts of Lilith with her copper curls glinting beneath the sun, flying out behind her as they raced to Cameron Castle, came back to haunt him. She rode with fierceness, laughed with abandon, and he knew without knowing she would love as wildly. Edan angrily put an end to his capricious thoughts. 'Twas impossible—he would not take her in a marriage of convenience.

"Angus! Speed, man, put on some speed." Edan made haste to outrun his longing.

****

When Lily finally ambled over the cool, wind-swept moors, deeply absorbed with the breathtaking scenery, it was mid-afternoon. The beautiful golden and rust hues of autumn blanketed the landscape. She marveled at the magnificent sight of the distant Caledonian Pine Forest. The peace of being home warmed her.

When she came to an old birch tree, the spot seemed perfect. She sat beneath its sheltering branches, spread her skirts and prepared to sketch birds. Looking back over her shoulder, she was surprised to find she could no longer see the manor. She'd wandered a mile or more from Glen Carin without even realizing. Lost in the natural beauty of the Highlands, she'd lost all sense of time and distance.

Scotland was home to several species of birds she did not often see in London, and she'd been on the lookout ever since leaving her old home. As if he had been summoned by Lily's muse, a handsome Red Kite swooped in to land in a nearby birch. Her charcoal stick flew over the blank white page of her sketch pad as she outlined the small head, feather-thick body and long tail feathers of the bird of prey.

Sketching always calmed her. But more than the peace the birds brought, she meant to escape through her sketches if she found no other way. She felt an affinity for birds of all kinds, slightly envious of their ability to take flight and be free of all earthly constraints. Unbeknownst to Lady Frances, Lily had deposited a book of bird sketches with a London publisher shortly before she left for Scotland.

There were few paths for a woman to become independent, the most notable being a writer like Jane Porter or Jane Austin. Did she dare hope the publishing company might purchase her illustrations? Such good fortune might free Charlotte and her from their mother's tyranny if Edan rejected her. A cold shudder ripped through Lily's body. No! The laird simply could not reject her!

Throwing off disturbing thoughts of what Lady Frances might do—including selling Lily off after Charlotte, she concentrated on sketching the kite. So engrossed in her work, Lily did not notice the band of men approaching until she felt the ground shaking beneath her and heard the thunder of horses' hooves. By then the small band were close upon her, frightening the graceful Red Kite which flapped its wings and flew away.

Putting aside her pad and charcoal stick, Lily rose, expecting to greet Edan and his brothers. But as the small band drew closer, trepidation snaked through her. She did not recognize one among the group. The six dirty, full-bearded men appeared menacing in every way, from their side-arms of muskets and dirks to their flinty-eyed, hostile expressions. The leader, astride a large, dappled mare, stopped only a few feet away from her.

The dust from the horses choked her. The fine

downy hairs on Lily's arms rose in warning. Alarmed, her heart raced. And then she remembered Edan's warning to not stray far from Glen Carin.

Too late.

Chapter 6

The leader of the ragtag band, whose black beard matched his closely-set black eyes and full spikey brows, leaned forward. "Who are ye, foolish lass?"

His rancid scent gagged her. She raised her chin. "I am…I am Lilith Munro, daughter of Rob Munro."

The words tumbled from her mouth without thought. She had not identified herself as Rob Munro's bairn since she was a child, but at the moment it felt right. She was Lily Munro, Highland lass, and would be until the day came when she was forced to leave Scotland.

The leader gave a disgusted grunt. "Rob Munro?" he asked, gathering his wayward brows into a frown that formed the two into one thick, dark downward slash between his eyes. "The once Laird of Glen Carin?"

She tilted her chin a bit higher. "Aye."

The man spat to the side of his horse. "Munro is dead and gone long since. What brings ye onto me land, Mistress Munro?"

"Your land?" She felt certain the land belonged to Edan.

"Aye," he growled, dismounting. "Did you no' hear me no'?" He pointed to the ground. "'Tis my land."

"I…I did not think this was your property. 'Tis

Cameron land."

"Yer mistaken." He spat again. "Badly."

Lily held up her sketch pad. "I was sketching the kite, the bird you frightened away." She swallowed the lump of fear stuck in her throat. "Who...who might you be?"

"Brodie."

"You have my apologies for trespassing," she said, turning from Edan's neighboring enemy and quickly snatching up her charcoals. "I shall leave at once."

"No' so fast." Quickly dismounting, Brodie seized Lily by her upper arm and spun her around to face him.

Facing him proved most unpleasant. He stood too close, and his breath smelled like a London gutter. "Mebbe I should hang ye as I would any man caught on me land." Brodie's upper lip curled in a menacing manner; a smile that wasn't a smile but rather a promise of pain.

"No!" she cried, wrestling out of his clutches. Although small in stature, Brodie proved to be strong. "I've...I've not done anything more than make a...a slight mistake."

"Besides, ye sound more English than Scot," he interrupted. His eyes, black as coal, flashed with hostility. "Sassenach," he snarled.

She watched with mounting terror as he spat on the ground beside her.

"English are no' welcome in the Highlands. We hang the likes of ye."

Ignoring her knocking knees, Lily held her head high and attempted to reason with the living gargoyle. "Please sir, I can see you are an honorable man and will excuse my error this one time. And do not let my accent deceive you. You well know Scots blood runs through my veins. Munro blood is thicker than the mist on the moors, 'tis."

"Aye? Then mebbe instead of hanging ye, I'll give ye a good bedding, no'?"

His men broke out in bawdy laughter.

The blood froze in her veins. Lily shuddered. All six of the blackguards hooted and howled as if Brodie had made the richest joke they'd ever heard. She felt the blood drain from her face. But showing fear would be the worst thing she could do. She considered making a run for it, but except for Brodie, the ruffians were on horseback and would catch her before she'd fled more than a yard.

"Ye are a pretty wench. Aye, I should take ye here and now, and when I am done with ye, I'll pass ye along to each of my men." Brodie leaned in even closer to Lily. He lowered his voice to a harsh whisper, as if he were sharing a secret. "'Tis been a long time since the lads have had a fine woman's touch."

Her heart pounded with fear. Her knees went from solid rock to runny custard, ready to give way. "Please—"

Just as she was about to disgrace herself and resort to begging, gunshots rang out. The sound and smoky fury of muskets and pocket pistols filled the once quiet glen.

She turned as one with Brodie's men to see the three Cameron brothers charging toward them. Edan raced ahead on his huge gelding.

The Cameron brothers were outnumbered two to one, but their unworldly battle cries and the volley of gunshots they managed made it sound as if a legion of men were bearing down on the small Brodie band.

"Bah!" Brodie spat again. "'Tis the English-lovin' laird and his brathers comin' to save the lass. We'll stand to fight another time." He narrowed his black gaze on Lily. His lips twisted into a lecherous smile. "Let this be a warning, lassie. Stay off Brodie property unless ye want me makin' love to ye on the rocky moors."

Laughing like a demented soul, he jumped on his mount, jerked on the reins, and turned to the south.

Shaking from head to toe, Lily watched as the devil's band galloped away chased by Angus and Finn, shouting epitaphs not meant for a lady's ears. Brodie's sinister laughter seemed to echo on the wind. As his laughter died away, the rapid tattoo of her wildly beating heart was all she heard.

Edan reined in his big black horse at her side. His disheveled hair fell to his shoulders unbound. Fury darkened his eyes to the color of night. "What do ye think you're doing?" he demanded with a sharpness that surprised her. She'd expected him to offer comfort. She required comfort!

"Did I no tell ye no to stray from Glen Carin?" he demanded.

"Ye…yes, but I did not realize how far I had gone. And I did not understand the danger." Once again she found herself raising her chin in defiance. "You failed to warn me!"

"I failed to warn ye?" He gritted the words between his teeth.

"You neglected to mention Brodie specifically."

A muscle ticked in his jaw. He laid down his reins to make room for her on his mount. "Get yer arse up here."

"Get up here?" she repeated, incensed. *Did he say arse?*

"What are ye waitin' for?"

"I thought you might have learned some drawing room manners, but I see I was mistaken."

He glared at her in a most ominous way. "Do no' be arguing with me."

Lily dug in her heels. "I am only stating the facts so that we are clear. I believed I was on your land when I sat down to sketch."

Leaning over toward her, Edan held out a hand to help Lily mount. "Ye *are* on Cameron land. But ye have strayed too far from Glen Carin to be safe from Brodie."

"Apparently," she sniffed, ignoring his hand.

"Come," he ordered, with a curt gesture of his head.

"You wish me to ride with you?"

"Get ye behind me, or get ye in front of me, but get ye up on my mount."

Lily couldn't believe he was ordering about as if she were a servant or...a wife. Turning to her sketch pad and box of charcoals, she objected. "But my things…"

"What things?"

"My sketch pad and—"

"Angus will bring them."

Lily stalled, staring at his outstretched hand.

"Bloody hell, Lilith!" he shouted. "Take my hand."

With one effortless motion, as if she weighed no more than her box of charcoal sticks, Edan pulled her up to sit before him on the giant steed.

Riding within an inch of the enticing laird's massive chest gave her pause. She knew not exactly why. Shifting uneasily, she regained her composure.

"Thank you," she sniffed, adjusting her skirts. Edan's hands, she noted, were warm, powerful hands.

"Ye are the most stubborn of Scot lasses," he mumbled beneath his breath.

"I heard that."

He growled low in his throat.

In the protective shadow of Edan's massive form, Lily found herself struggling for breath. Tension emanated from his steely body as he settled in the saddle. She may have underestimated the time she needed at Glen Carin to win him over. The laird might possibly be as stubborn as she. Admittedly, to date her plan had not gone exactly as…planned.

And then with one subtle movement of his knees, Edan urged his magnificent horse toward Glen Carin Manor.

****

The chill of the day deepened, caught, and carried in a raw wind. Winter was on its way.

Bone deep fear ripped through Edan when he'd seen Lily surrounded by Brodie and his men. His blood turned to ice. On the battlefield he'd feared for his life, but he'd never experienced the raw terror that gripped him upon discovering Lily's life in danger. His every muscle and marrow burned with dread. The roar of his heart overrode the sound of his big horse's hooves as he'd raced to her rescue.

When at last he arrived at the spot where Lilith stood, head held high, the knot in his gut tightened at the sight of her. Tension coursed through his body. Her spring-green eyes were wide with fright and strands of her sunset hair, unleashed by the wind, framed her pale face in a wild tangle. Her lips trembled.

His heart constricted.

But now, with Lilith safe upon his horse, he could breathe again. His arms reached around her to take the reins and guide the animal home. He set Dragon to a slow pace. For no understandable reason, a sense of well-being began to flow through Edan, replacing his fears. He savored the warm nearness of Lilith's body, inhaled the sweet rose scent of her hair. And a searing primal need swept through him, a need that could never be met. No matter how reckless Lilith was, she deserved a better man than he.

"How long have you been feuding with Brodie?" she asked, breaking the silence.

"For as long as I can remember. If it is no' one thing, 'tis another. Some men enjoy the fight. At present the Brodies have no use for our sheep. They claim Cameron sheep wander onto their farmland and damage their crops."

"You might have warned me about him."

"Ye might have mentioned you would stray away in order to sketch a pigeon."

"'Twas a Red Kite, not a pigeon! And sketching is what I enjoy. Other women knit and needlework. I sketch."

"You would do better to take up needlework. 'Tis safer," he snapped.

"But boring."

Edan sensed a need to change the conversation. "Have ye finished plans for the ceilidh?"

"Nay."

Edan felt grateful for the distraction conversation with Lilith offered. He willed the fire she'd stirred within him to cool and damned himself for being weak, for he ached with need. These past months he'd been entirely consumed with restoring the Cameron land. He could not even recall how long it had been since he'd had a woman, far too long, judging from his reaction to the nearness of the reckless redhead.

Lilith would not make the sort of wife he required, and worse, once married, her admiration for him would be destroyed. Admiration she did not hide and that he had begun to care about, oddly enough. He cared how Lily thought of him. Married to him as she'd proposed, she would discover the dark side he'd managed so far to hide from the world.

He would not be a good husband to Lilith or any woman. He must, and would marry, but only out of duty. Edan knew what no one else suspected; he'd inherited the black heart of his da. If he gave his heart, if he dared love a woman, over time she would be doomed to neglect and worse. Edan had learned well from his parent.

Lilith cut into his thoughts. Again. Apparently, the woman could not be silent. "I have no need to worry about safety when sketching in Hyde Park," she said in the same uppity tone she'd been using since he'd come to her rescue.

He grunted in response. "Then ye need to return to Hyde Park."

Despite his indifferent reply, a prickly feeling spread throughout his body. Pins and needles spiraled through his veins. Truth was the longer Lilith stayed, the more danger she was in—from him. He did not trust himself, did not trust the lust that stirred within and warmed him. The minx brushed against him, and the warmth became fire, the fire became desire.

He must turn down her proposal of marriage as soon as possible. As soon as she cried off from arranging the ceilidh. Which if he pressed her, took her to task, might be any hour now with a wee bit of luck. She would cry off with her pride intact. And his.

Edan urged his mighty gelding to a faster pace. The wind, cold and biting, accosted them even as a heavy mist rose up to circle around the riders.

"Why are we racing?" Lilith asked. Eden had tensed suddenly, and she wondered at the subtle change.

"Because 'tis cold and I have nothing to warm ye," he barked. "Best we return to Glen Carin as swiftly as possible."

The cold, damp, speed and gathering dusk surrounded the riders as the big horse, Dragon plunged toward home. Glen Carin.

****

Edan was wrong about having nothing to warm her.

Lily drew her pelisse closer. Edan's body offered the heat of four fires. Or more. Riding before him in the saddle, pressed against his hard, muscular chest, his closeness disconcerted her and caused her heart to flutter as if it had sprouted wings. Her breath came in ragged gasps.

Floundering, she searched for something to say, something to take her mind off the pleasure of his nearness, the leather and earthy scent of him. For just as when she was a girl, she wished for more. Then she had wished for more of his time and attention. As a woman, Lily yearned for Edan to take her in his arms and hold her tightly, hold her as if he would never let her go.

Too soon they approached Glen Carin. The brief ride and the intimacy Lily enjoyed with the heart-stopping laird ended. Edan pulled his horse, so appropriately named Dragon, to a stop in front of the stables. Lowering his head, he whispered in Lily's ear. His breath warmed her neck, causing a series of exquisite chills to skip down her spine. "If in the future ye should venture farther than the garden in pursuit of birds, be warned. I shall be sending ye and yer sister back to London before your maid can finish packing your trunk, Lilith Munro."

Edan Cameron threatened to send her packing! Lily could barely believe what she'd heard. She was an English lady and Scots born. No one had ever dared speak to her in that manner. Vexed beyond bounds, she curled her hands into fists. How dare he!

But he dared with yet another warning. "Dinna fash, Lilith."

"Och!" she cried in anger, reverting to the common. Before she could unleash the full force tongue lashing he so richly deserved, one of the stable boys hurried forward with a stool. The boy raised a hand to help her dismount.

With her feet planted on solid ground she huffed, "Good day, Laird Cameron."

Chuckling, Edan looked down upon her from his mount and flashed what could only be called a roguish expression. One corner of his mouth turned up in a bone-melting smile.

The man tormented her. Her feelings hurtled

between anger and desire and back to a slow burn, which might or might not be a good thing. Whirling on her heel, she stomped away to her bedchamber without a backward glance. No matter how he distressed her, Lily meant to marry the arrogant man. Acquiring Edan's protection with their arranged union was the most expeditious means to save Charlotte from an unacceptable marriage.

Certainly if Lily had known the danger the Brodies posed, she would have stayed in the garden. Did Edan think her a nitwit?

The cold, tight-lipped laird who had come to her rescue was a far cry from the caring young man of her memory. Back then, when Edan was beyond the sight and hearing of his father, he'd always had a twinkle in his eyes for her. He'd teased the young Lily regularly, pulling her braid and tweaking her nose. And when she stomped her foot in indignation, he would throw his head back and laugh, a deep rumbling belly laugh that despite her irritation made her smile. It had been impossible to remain angry with a man who seemingly laughed from the depths of his soul. Lily had not heard Edan laugh, really laugh, since her arrival.

As angry unspoken words for the dark laird swirled in her head, her body remained warm from the heat he'd radiated on the ride home. And his departing grin was excessively irritating.

Soon she was soaking away the cold in a tepid bath. Somehow the water was never hot by the time it arrived at the tub. The copper tub sat by the fireplace. Netta had responded to Lily's request with many a *tsk-tsk* and mutterings about what becomes of a woman who bathes too much. As soon as Netta left the bedchamber, Lily slid deeper into the water. A shudder ripped through her at the thought of running into Edan's ruthless neighbor Brodie again. She considered the wisdom of acquiring a weapon, something she hadn't required in London, but appeared evident she might require in the Highlands. Edan had enemies. His enemies were now hers. Dare she ask Edan to supply her with a weapon?

After her bath, with her maid Jane's help, Lily changed into an emerald silk dinner gown and knocked on Charlotte's door.

"Who is it?"

"Lily, you silly sister."

"Come in."

Charlotte reclined on a chaise, still wearing the same dressing gown she had that morning.

"'Tis time for you to dress, Charlotte, and come with me to supper. You will enjoy the company of the Cameron brothers. You cannot stay locked away for our entire visit."

"Has the laird not responded yet to your proposal?"

"Not yet."

"I knew this scheme would not go well."

"You know he has asked that we plan the gala and demonstrate drawing room manners to him and his brothers. I feel his requests are a step in the right direction. The more responsibility given to me, the longer we must stay. He must wish for me to stay. I am making inroads into his heart."

"Unbeknownst to him, I fear! The laird is taking advantage of your good nature," Charlotte said, angling her head and touching a finger to her chin as if in deep thought. "Or perhaps he is taking advantage of your willingness to do anything to hear him say aye to your proposal."

"You may be right. I expect either way makes no difference."

Charlotte heaved a sigh and twittered like an old woman. "I agreed to help with the gala, and I will, Lily. I do understand you are only attempting to help me."

Lily gave her sister a smile, a bit doleful, she knew. "Attempting is the key word."

"When you first proposed your plan, I thought you were making a great sacrifice on my behalf. However, when first I saw how handsome the laird is, I changed my mind. Any woman would be thrilled to marry Edan Cameron."

"He is also a stern, stubborn, and overbearing Highlander. Appearance is not everything."

Charlotte's pursed lips slid into a smile. "You have had an argument with him."

Lily released a whoosh of a sigh. "Will you come with me? Following supper, we will teach the Cameron brothers how to waltz."

She shook her head, blond curls bounced in her firm denial. "Perhaps tomorrow."

"Maisie will be here tomorrow to help us prepare for the ceilidh. There will be no time for dancing."

A vague look of disinterest shadowed Charlotte's expression as she nodded. "I promise I shall join you and Maisie for the gala planning."

The battle was over, Lily knew. A bit of the Scot stubborn ran through Charlotte's veins as well. She would not change her mind. "Until the morrow, then. Goodnight, sweet."

Her spoiled younger sister's continued obstinacy

and Edan's endless indifference annoyed Lily immensely. It was all she could do to smile as she entered the dining hall. Her smile faded swiftly.

Only Netta greeted her in the empty hall. "Good evening, Netta."

"Laird Cameron waits on ye in the parlor," she replied tersely.

Edan wanted to see her. Lily's heart skipped. One beat. Two beats. The time had come. He'd never summoned her before. He must be ready to agree to her marriage proposal. When the laird asked for one's company, one complied. "I'll see him in the parlor straightaway, as soon as I have freshened up."

Humming happily, Lily rushed back to her bedchamber, purposefully delaying the inevitable—a marriage agreement between Edan and her. She asked Jane to brush her hair. Following a brushing that left her mass of copper curls shining, she staged a slow search for a silk shawl to wrap around her shoulders.

Smiling and feeling a bit smug inside, she glided into the parlor almost an hour later, but not only Edan waited for her. Angus and Finn waited with him. Each of the brothers reclined in a separate area of the room and each met Lily's arrival with a smile. 'Twas like a dream. Three extraordinarily handsome men regarded her as if she had just hung the moon. Edan was the most striking, in her opinion—and in her heart. Even if he did take pleasure in tormenting her.

But then, she noticed, with some apprehension, the furniture had been removed from the center of the room and the faded Aubusson carpet had been rolled up and set aside.

Edan greeted her with a lazy grin. "Lilith, 'tis time

to teach auld Angus the waltz."

Angus bounded up from the dainty Sheraton chair where he'd been sitting and planted his fists on his hips.

Lily caught the slight quiver at the corner of Edan's mouth as he nodded. "The time is near when my brothers and I will be invited into the drawing rooms of the Edinburgh elite and the English aristocracy. We canna no' delay any longer. We would appreciate yer help in polishing our social graces."

Which very well might take the rest of her life.

"I shall do my best."

But when she approached Angus, she came up short. "You need to bathe," she declared, wrinkling her nose.

"I dinna ken." The big man scowled. "I washed four days ago."

"If you ever wish to find yourself a wife, you'll bathe every day."

"Every day!" he repeated. "Then I dinna need a wife."

"But you do need to wash and wear clean clothes if you expect to be welcome in country homes and drawing rooms. Especially if you expect me to teach you to dance."

"Yer no' the Lilith I remember. Yer a Sassenach!" he accused her, in an angry tone.

"You will also need to shave occasionally."

His mouth dropped open. "I dinna need to waltz," he declared, stomping out the door. "Nor shave," he called out over his shoulder.

Looking after him, Lily shook her head. She disliked making Angus angry, but even more she disliked the stable smell of him.

"He'll learn to bathe on a regular basis," Edan assured her.

Finn stood. "I promise not to offend ye, Lilith."

She approached the quiet, serious Cameron brother with a smile. "I shall be glad to demonstrate the steps. But…" Lily looked to Edan. "But what shall we do for music?"

"Hum," Edan replied.

"Hum?"

"You hum a great deal. I hear ye humming."

"Yes, well…" Lily glanced at the pianoforte in the corner. Years ago, she had learned to play on the beautiful instrument that now collected dust. Lily used to play "The Blue Bell of Scotland" for her father, singing along with the haunting lyrics. Delicately played, the music provided hours of comfort to her da as he lay dying.

Hot tears stung behind her eyes.

"Why is the waltz considered daring?" Finn asked.

"Well, because…" Lily tamped down her tears. How could she explain to Finn? Her cheeks grew hot with embarrassment. "…Because the dance partners, um, touch, each other." Exceedingly uncomfortable, she looked to Edan for help.

He appeared bemused as his gaze locked on hers, pining Lily to the spot. Her awareness of the man, the one-time warrior and the leader of his people heightened in the silence. Her admiration intensified. Dressed for super, his broad, square shoulders and wide chest threatened to stretch the clean white linen shirt he wore. His fawn breeches fit snugly against muscular thighs.

Thankfully, Edan came to her rescue, answering

Lily's silent plea. "I shall be yer first partner. Watch and learn, Finn."

Lily smiled nervously. "Um, place your hand on my waist, so."

The warmth of Edan's hand burned through her silk gown. She felt the heat down to her toes. By the stoic look on Edan's face he felt nothing. His gaze centered somewhere above Lily's head.

"I shall place one hand on your shoulder, and we will clasp hands, thusly." She took his hand in hers, held it high and stepped back as far as possible. If they made bodily contact even by accident, she might swoon like a girl in her first season. "The count is important. Count silently in time with the music—"

Except there was no music.

"Would ye like me to play my pipes?" Angus asked. He'd returned to the parlor, flashing his cheerful grin. His anger forgotten. 'Twas his way, Lily recalled.

"Thank you, but the waltz cannot be danced to the bagpipe."

"Then how good can this dance be, no'?"

"We will show ye," she said. "It begins with the count. One, two, three, Edan. One, two, three."

With the laird's warm hand on her back, his hand enveloping hers, he guided Lily into the dance She knew immediately that he had waltzed before. Why should she be surprised? He gracefully danced her across the room under the watchful eyes of his brothers. Dizzy and out of breath before she knew it, Lily could not stop smiling. Her happy heart felt near to bursting. She and Edan danced as if they had danced together for many years. Why did he not respond to her proposal of marriage when dancing with him, being in his arms seemed so right? If nothing else, they could dance their way through life.

Edan's eyes never met hers. His gaze remained over her head with just a nod to his brothers now and again. Lily's heart fluttered just as it had years ago when she was a silly schoolgirl, adoring him from afar. The laird was so very masculine. So very powerful.

At last he slowed and stopped. "Finn, come dance with Lilith."

Finn appeared uncertain so Lily opened her arms and grinned. "You are like a brother to me, and you are a Highlander. Do not fear the dance."

For an hour more, Lily danced with Finn and Angus. Angus stepped on her toes frequently, but he worked so hard at learning the steps and tempo she could not be angry.

Hungry and tired, the Cameron brothers made short work of dinner. Lily could not blame the men, for the day had been tiring for her as well in so many ways. Finn accompanied Lily to her bedchamber.

Exhausted, by the time she climbed into bed, Lily expected to fall asleep instantly. But no. Her thoughts of Edan, her proposal, the ceilidh she had yet to plan kept her awake. She required a book to take her mind off her worries and lull her to sleep. Something philosophical. Recalling her father had kept an extensive library, Lily threw off her covers, donned her dressing gown and with lantern held high, she left her bedchamber on tiptoe. Braving the cold floor, she made her way down the stairs and into the west wing corridor. She soon found the cozy chamber she remembered.

Thirty minutes later, Lily had found her da's

favorite book. He had loved his books; he had loved this library. Her heart raced as if she'd found him here in the musty chamber. She'd discovered his essence in just about every chamber in Glen Carin. How would she ever be able to leave again? Edan simply could not refuse to marry her.

She clasped the book to her chest, prepared to leave when she heard footsteps, caught sight of a giant shadow, and then the man. Lily froze. Edan stood in the doorway. Startled.

In the distance, the Longcase clock chimed two. Two o'clock in the morning. The chimes echoed through the manor.

****

Edan stood immobile, steadily regarding the vision before him. Was he dreaming? He seemed unable to avoid Lilith even in the deepest night. Unable to convey the reason for his unwillingness to marry her, he hesitated to be alone with the impudent lass. Yet in the cold dark chamber, he could not help staring at the beauty Lilith Munro had become. In the lantern light, her loveliness transfixed him. He filled his eyes, his senses with her. Her amazing mass of curls fell to her shoulders in a shining cinnamon cloud. Her full moist lips were the color of peaches and parted as if waiting for his kiss. The swell of her breasts warmed him, ignited a fire deep in his soul. His palms ached to touch, to caress her in intimate appreciation. But he had not the will to wound her. He refused to offer Lilith hope, to have her believe she would soon be his bride.

He moved to within a foot of her. "Lilith Munro, are ye lost?"

"Apparently I have been found."

He lowered his gaze to the curving outline of her hips beneath her dressing gown. Then, swiftly he raised his gaze to hers once more. The lush green of her dressing gown enhanced the jewel glow of her eyes. Unmoving, she did not appear to fear him. And she could not know how much she beguiled him. The longing he felt for her doubled into desire, a burning desire impossible to ignore.

"I could not sleep so I came to the library in search of a book," she explained.

The woman seemed unable to tolerate silence. At every turn she interrupted his thoughts, his feelings.

"You have found a book? What were ye looking for?"

"A book of poetry by Robert Burns. I was about to return to my chamber."

"Are you in a hurry, Lilith?"

"We are alone," she whispered. "We should not be alone." She took a step forward and a step to the side of him.

But he could not let her go. "Are ye not afraid of me?"

A flash of surprise widened her eyes. "Never. Why would I fear you?"

"Because I want ye. Because I am known for taking what I want."

Before she could say nay, Edan swept Lily into his arms and brought his mouth down on hers. His heart beat fiercely, and a fire unlike any he had never known swept through him at the honey taste of her lips.

Gradually, and ever so sweetly, her lips parted beneath his.

"Madness," a voice in his head called out.

"*Madness.*"

Edan struggled against a desire so fierce it frightened him in a manner he'd never been frightened before. During the bleakest moments on the battlefield and on the home front, he'd never wavered. But now...

Clasping Lilith's shoulders, he set her back from him. With his gaze riveted to hers, Edan attempted to read her thoughts whilst attempting to understand his feelings. *What in thunder had made him do that?* For a long, tense moment the agonized roar of his heart resounded in his ears. Caught in a dark wave of confusion, he turned on his heel and stalked away. He did not want, could not have Lilith.

Silence descended on the library, broken only by echoes of footsteps and distant calls of nocturnal creatures. Darkness mitigated slightly by lantern light, a shaky light, casting shadows.

Stunned and quite speechless, Lily watched the laird leave. Edan's deep, bruising kiss had all but stopped her heart. She had never been kissed with such...gusto. But then, she'd never been kissed.

Shivering, she stood alone in the chilly corridor. Would she ever wish to be kissed by any other man? Obviously, Edan was not indifferent to her. So why did he resist her? Resolved anew to compel the reluctant laird to agree to her proposal, Lily headed back to her bedchamber. Smiling as if she knew a secret, she drifted down the corridors on a cloud.

Chapter 7

He wanted her. He'd said he wanted her!

Lily's heart continued to dance long after she'd returned to bed and pulled the generous down covers up to her chin. She touched her lips, reliving his kiss. She imagined tracing the scar slashed across his cheek, softly kissing the angry wound. An unfamiliar tenderness, a warming, washed within her. But she could not linger on such thoughts.

If she did not receive a marriage agreement soon, poor Charlotte would be thrown to the wolf known as Whetfield. Tossing her book aside, Lily turned her thoughts to methods of seduction. Surely since Edan had admitted that he wanted her, she should be able to seduce him into marriage. Although she'd never attempted seduction, she'd heard gossip and learned of several methods that had been used to woo reluctant suitors. But was seduction honest? Was it right?

His kiss had told her "Aye!" Yes, it was.

Furthermore, forcing Charlotte into marrying old, evil Whetfield wasn't right. Such an arrangement was distressingly wrong but would come to pass if Lily did not take whatever action was necessary. She smiled to herself. She rather thought she would enjoy seducing Edan. A kiss? A subtle brush of her body against his? Several times. At last, she closed her eyes and drifted into a peaceful slumber.

****

In another bedchamber a slice of golden moonlight slipped through a gap in the worn drapes. The fire, burning low, crackled within a comforting concert of night sounds. All seemed well beneath the roof of Glen Carin.

Except that Edan slept fitfully. The honeyed taste of Lilith's lips remained on his. He hadn't expected her lips to be so sweet. He hadn't expected her warm response to his kiss or to be shaken to his core. But what did he actually know of Rob Munro's comely daughter now?

Anyone could see Lilith was exceptionally beautiful and possessed a quick, intelligent mind. Although he wondered if a quick intelligent mind might not be a truly desirable quality in a wife. Still, he was forced to concede, if only to himself, a marriage of convenience with Lilith might serve both of their purposes. She would be safely away from Lady Frances, and living with him in the Highlands, and he could, as Lilith requested, provide his protection to Charlotte. Both from her mother and the arranged marriage both the sisters wished to avoid.

He was a farmer. A farmer was all he had ever wanted to be. At last he'd achieved his dream so long hidden from his da and brothers. At present he could not support the life of a lady from the ton. Even though he worked to restore his estate wealth, at present Edan could only offer his protection, provide shelter and as many meals as the lasses could consume.

For one, Lilith possessed a hearty appetite. She also appeared to enjoy a growing fondness for the ale. Most importantly, there was no need to court the bold lass. Lilith appeared smitten with him from the day she'd arrived with her startling proposal.

Still the "old" Lilith returned to haunt him. Could he trust this "new" lass? Already she'd defied him by straying from the manor and nearly being abducted by Brodie. Lilith might still harbor the reckless trait she demonstrated as a child. Had she changed? Really changed?

On the positive side, her heart was as big as the North Sea. He also knew Lilith would never shirk responsibility. Even as a child, she had helped in the fields and with the horses. She'd never failed to jump into a fray or nay say to a request.

This rocky, craggy country was hers as well as his and the love of it shone in her smile. While many a woman had run from the cruel climate of the Highlands, the misty chill brought roses to her cheeks. Most probably Lilith could give him something he desired even more than profitable Cameron land. She could give him a son, a strong, healthy heir.

Sleep evaded Edan. He tossed and turned and could not let go of the thought of an arranged marriage. He would be a fool to allow her to leave. His brothers thought of Lilith's propitious arrival at Glen Carin as a gift—though he hadn't been of like mind. Was it only days ago? Tonight, he couldn't help feeling she was meant to be his. But he had nothing to offer the daughter of a beloved and respected chief, nothing but life as a farmer's wife. Struggling with these unfamiliar feelings stirred by Lilith; Edan worried he might be unable to overcome the black heart legacy left by his da.

Early the next morning, Edan met up with Angus

and Finn to pay a visit to Brodie. He was about to deliver his last warning. If Brodie came near his land or his woman again, the Cameron brothers would burn Brodie crops down to the ground.

"When are ye going to ask Lilith to marry ye?" Angus wanted to know before they'd traveled more than a mile.

Still mired in confusion and frustration regarding what to do about Rob Munro's daughter, Edan wasn't prepared to share his thoughts with his brothers. "Perhaps I shall meet a stranger at the ceilidh who will capture my fancy. A woman not known to be a hellion."

"Lady Frances willna like it one bit if ye marry her lass," Angus mused with a broad grin. Anything to upset Lady Frances was a good thing in the mind of all the Cameron brothers.

Edan shook his head. "I have nothing to offer Lilith."

"Aye, but nothing is a temporary condition," his burly brother observed. "Besides, the lass might be of a different mind. Lilith's been sweet on ye since she was just a wee one. Aye, and before long our pockets will be full again, no?"

"Do you think Lilith is truly willing to marry you and remain in the Highlands?" Finn asked, always practical, requiring only facts. Before Edan could answer he offered another notion. "The lass may soon discover that she prefers the less rigorous life she's been living in London. Have you considered the possibility? She may have behaved impulsively on behalf of her sister and even now regretting her actions. Women are known to be hopeless romantics."

"Lilith does no' seem a romantic," Edan snapped,

hoping to put an end to Finn's analysis. "From early on she's taken great pleasure in torturing me."

"What ye be needin' is our help in wooin' the lass," Angus declared with a wink.

"No," Edan replied quickly, "I dinna need your help." The thought of Angus helping him to court the redheaded beauty was enough to give him an aching head. She had already suggested they marry with no courting involved. A proposition he had not seriously considered until recent sleepless nights. He shook his head as if to shake all thoughts of Lilith from his mind. "Enough of Lilith. Let us put our minds to the business at hand and strike the fear of Camerons in the Brodie clan."

Angus raised his arm and shook his fist. "Aye, I'll be fierce."

"In the past Brodie has proven to be a dunderheid. He does no' listen well," Finn said with a frustrated wag of his head.

"He will listen today." Edan gritted his teeth, narrowed his eyes. "Brodie will stay off our land and away from the sheep or we will come down upon him and his clan like the Campbells at Glencoe." Although doing it a bit too strong, he succeeded in turning his brothers' attention to the task at hand.

****

Gray skies darkened and a cold mist blanketed the Highland hills. The distant stark mountains rose like centurions to guard farms, thatched cottages, castles, and manors. It was a day like most fall days.

Lily knocked on Charlotte's chamber. "Sweet, we have little time left to us. Four days."

"Four days? It cannot be done."

"It must be. Although Edan moved the ceilidh forward, I must prove to him that I can make his celebration a success with only a very little time."

"It cannot be done," Charlotte repeated.

"Netta's daughter, Maisie is here to help us."

Charlotte opened the door just enough to peek around it. "Even you cannot assemble a ball in four days, Lily."

"'Tis not a ball. The ceilidh is more like a gala and success can be achieved with your help and Maisie's. She waits for us in the parlor," Lily told her sister gently. "Maisie is your age and appears to have a constant smile. I'm certain you shall like her."

"Where is the laird?"

"He and his brothers have left on business of some sort."

"Has he agreed to wed you?"

Lily cleared her dry throat. "Edan is a cautious man as a laird should be. I suspect he is waiting for the ceilidh success before he agrees. What better time to celebrate? Now, come." 'Twas neither the answer Charlotte wished to hear, nor the answer Lily wished to give.

"Dear Sister," Charlotte rested a sad-eyed gaze on Lily. "I fear you may misjudge the laird."

"No. No, no. I have not," Lily insisted, refusing to concede. "Now, come."

With a roll of her eyes, Charlotte took Lily's hand and allowed her sister to lead her from the refuge of her bedchamber.

Maisie stood by the fireplace with her hands clasped in front of her. The housekeeper's daughter owned a round pleasant figure. Her brown eyes were large, and deep dimples signaled a young woman who smiled often. She appeared nervous but shoved her hands in the pockets of her apron and smiled brightly as Lily and Charlotte entered the parlor.

"We are so pleased to have your help, Maisie. This is my sister Charlotte who will work with us."

"I've never planned a gala," Charlotte said, springing to her own defense before necessary.

Maisie grinned, showing a gap where a bottom tooth should have been. "Dinna fash. We'll put on a good time."

Lily ushered the girls to a small table beneath one of the windows. "Let us sit and plan. Where do you suggest we begin, Maisie?"

"The great hall will need to be cleaned. My mather will call in help. We'll post a notice in the village that a ceilidh is to be held at Glen Carin on whatever the given day. Musicians will come from the village as well as the townspeople. Word will spread quickly to all the neighboring farms. Before the sun goes down on ceilidh day, the garden and great hall will be filled with music and dancing.

"Should we serve refreshments?" Lily asked.

"Aye. My mather will see to the feast. She knows the best cooks in the village, and each will bring her best dish to the ceilidh. 'Tis what is done in the Highlands for Hogmanay or any celebration."

Charlotte's expression spoke of relief. "There appears little for us to do."

"There is something…"

Lily brightened. "What would that be?"

"The laird provides the ale. Much ale."

Lily drew a deep breath. The expenses were

quickly mounting, and she knew the laird had financial worries. Edan must pay for the ale, the cleaning help, and the refreshments. "Perhaps we could clean and clear out the hall ourselves."

"Sister, are you serious?" Charlotte asked, her blue eyes wide with horror or disbelief. Lily could not be certain.

"Aye," Lily assured her with a grin.

"No. Not I!"

"Why not?" Anger and frustration toward her spoiled sister stirred within Lily.

Before Charlotte could answer, Maisie spoke up. "Charlotte and I might pay a visit on the MacDonald's. They make most of the ale and whiskey in this part of the Highlands."

"Would such a visit be dangerous?"

"Nay." Maisie shook her head of tight, auburn curls. "'Tis a guid ride of a hoor or so."

"Please, Lily. I have been imprisoned for days. And I have not ridden for weeks." Charlotte exchanged smiles with Maisie. "I trust Maisie."

Dumfounded, Lily agreed, for it was step in the right direction for her sister. "Only if several of the laird's men accompany you," she stipulated.

Charlotte readily consented, "As many men as you wish."

Maisie smiled broadly. "We shall leave early on the morrow, Miss Charlotte."

"I shall be ready."

"Good." A rush of excitement streamed through Lily. "We know what to do and have no time to waste. Let's start straight away by clearing the great hall."

"Now? I am not dressed to…to clear furniture."

"Sweet, today you will supervise while Maisie and I move the furnishings and rugs. We'll leave the tapestries."

Lily literally rolled up her sleeves to work with Maisie while Charlotte sat on a stool pointing out spider webs and dust balls. By days end, Lily was exhausted, and her sister had long before retired for a nap.

"We still need cleaning supplies for my mather's work tomorrow," Maisie told Lily at the end of the day. "The rags and such are locked in the outside storeroom."

"She doesn't have the key?" Lily asked.

Maisie shook her head.

"Does she know where the key might be?"

"The laird keeps the key in his bedchamber for safekeeping."

"Oh." Lily understood that storeroom keys were often kept from the servants until supplies were needed. The common practice cut down on thievery. Not that she believed Netta to be a thief.

Lily had no inkling of if and when she might see Edan before supper. Gathering the cleaning supplies now would help get an early start in the morning. "I will fetch the key and bring it to your mother. You have worked gallantly today, Maisie. Go home and rest. Tomorrow will also be tiring, I fear."

Lily hurried to the second level of the manor with mixed emotions. Fear of discovery and excitement of entering an off-limits chamber pumped her heart to a near racing speed. She meant to act quickly and search for the Doonie Purse while she fetched the coveted keys. She would be in and out of Eden's chamber without him ever knowing she'd been in his private retreat.

The Longcase clock chimed out the hour. She must do what she had to do. She entered Edan's chamber slowly, humming softly to cover her nervousness. It seemed to Lily that she was doing a lot of humming lately. The door creaked behind her. She stood for a moment, allowing her eyes to adjust to the darkness.

She had been here before. She knew this spacious room. Her breath caught in her throat. This had been her father's bedchamber. The heavy navy velvet drapes in Edan's spacious bedchamber were drawn causing the room to be dark even though it was still light beyond the lead windows. Lily pushed the drapes back from all three of the floor to ceiling windows before she could consider beginning her search.

Edan, as laird, enjoyed the finest dark mahogany Sheraton furnishings, including a bed so large three men could sleep in peace and an intricately carved washstand. An enormous stone fireplace covered one wall. From the looks of the flickering embers, a fire was kept burning at all times.

Adjoining the bedchamber an arched door opened onto a sitting room with a desk, bookshelves, and a settee covered with a deep burgundy embroidered fabric. The oriental carpet was the same as that in the bedchamber.

Lily felt like a thief. A series of cold chills trickled down her spine as she approached Edan's desk. The wide plank floor creaked beneath her leather slippers. She looked over her shoulder. The solid door remained shut.

She opened and combed through the two desk drawers without finding the key. No keys. Any keys.

And no Doonie Purse. She took her search to the bookshelves where she knew cautious people hid important papers and keys between the pages of books. She had removed one thick volume of the famous English writer, Shakespeare, and found success. A ring of keys lay behind the book. At least a dozen keys hung on the ring. Surely, she thought, one must open the storeroom. She snatched up the ring and shoved it into her pocket. 'Twas then she heard the door to the bedchamber open.

She stiffened.

"Bring me a bath," Edan shouted.

Lily made a dash to hide behind the sitting room door.

"Who in bloody hell opened these drapes?"

She was trapped.

Lily held her breath. She listened to the whoosh as he drew the drapes, plunging the room into semi-darkness once more.

Next, a parade of servants marched into the bedchamber.

Her stomach lurched.

"Set the tub down close to the fire," Edan ordered.

She peeked around the door hoping she could dash out with whatever servants had delivered the tub. But it was not to be. Three more men entered the chamber, each carrying two buckets of steaming water.

Pulse racing, she ducked back behind the door.

After several moments, Edan issued his final command. "Close the door behind you."

Lily's heart hammered nonstop. She had trouble drawing breath. What had happened to the air? Clasping her hands together, she could only hope the laconic laird would quickly bathe and dress and hurry down to supper with his brothers.

All was quiet. Tension spiraled through her body. For a moment she thought her heart had stopped. What was Edan doing?

Unable to stand the suspense, once again, she peeked round the corner. The back of the tub was to the door where she was hiding, and it was empty. She ducked back.

Lily felt a desperate need to run. Or pace. Or hum. Or something.

The palms of her hands had gone clammy. Ever so quietly, she clasped them together.

And at last she heard what sounded like a boot drop to the floor. Thud.

And then another. Thud.

Unable to contain her curiosity, she peeked around once again.

Mother Have Mercy! She should not be seeing what she was seeing, but Lily could not look away for the life of her. Her gaze fixed on his body,

From years of hard labor and war, thick muscles defined his back but also the ravaging scars from those long-ago beatings from his father. The faded tracks of his da's whip brought tears to her eyes. She ached to soothe Edan's scars.

When he began to push down his trousers, Lily knew she should close her eyes, but found it impossible. His trim waist widened down to firm, tight buttocks. Dark curls sprinkled over the muscular calves of his legs. If he turned, she dared not think what she might see and how she might react.

She was close to swooning when he entered the

tub, one long muscled leg after another. From where Lily stood, his manhood was safely out of sight. But she'd seen enough to whet her curiosity.

Please do not let me sneeze now, she prayed.

Standing in the darkness of the sitting room watching as Edan washed his body and then his hair, Lily longed to help the splendidly constructed laird. Drops of water glistened on his loose raven locks and sun-leathered shoulders.

And then, much to Lily's dismay, he rested his head on the high back of the tub. Was he about to go to sleep? She could not see his eyes through the back of his head. Were they closed? Were they open? Did his apparent respite offer the opportunity to escape?

She decided to take the risk. 'Twas now or never. Mustering her courage and taking a deep breath, she hurtled toward the main chamber door as fast as possible on tiptoes. The floor creaked beneath her just as she reached for the door latch.

"Are ye leaving so soon, Lilith?"

Chapter 8

Lily froze.

"'Tis only one reason why ye have come to my bedchamber, no?"

"No. I am…I did not come…I found myself in the wrong, the wrong chamber," she stammered. Her eye twitched madly.

"Do ye confuse me for an eejit?"

"No. No, of course not."

"I have just washed away a day's worth of grime and sheep. If yer interested, and yer presence indicates ye are, I'm prepared to demonstrate how a Highlander makes love."

Lily stared at the door handle. Her cheeks burned. "I…I…my apologies for intruding."

"Turn around."

She could not mistake the command. Anger and embarrassment warred in the pit of her stomach. She turned slowly.

Edan rose out of the water and stood. Droplets of water clung to his body in heart-stopping fashion. His manhood, in all its glory, seemed to stand at attention just for her. She meant to look away. She meant to close her eyes. But her marveling gaze never wavered. She absolutely could not look away. Fierce, demanding warmth stirred deep within her.

Where to look?

She hummed.

"…where is your Highland laddie gone?" Edan gave a snort.

Oh, no! Had she just hummed a piece of the "Blue Bell of Scotland" aloud?

The laird grinned, obviously enjoying her distress. "Hand over the blanket, Lilith."

Discomfort abruptly gave way to indignation. "I am not your servant!" she cried.

"But ye would be my wife."

"Not the same thing!" Picking up the blanket and turning away, Lily threw it his direction.

She heard the splash.

And his reaction. "Och!"

'Twas time to make a getaway. Opening the door, she ran down the corridor to her bedchamber. She slammed the door closed and flattened her body against it, breathing heavily. Lily knew she would never be able to look at the hero of her youth in the same way.

A small smile worked its way onto her lips.

****

Two days later on the eve before the ceilidh, Lily felt calm and exceedingly confident of presiding over a successful gala. The great hall waited scrubbed and spacious, and Maisie and Charlotte had completed business at the MacDonalds. The girls had gathered copious amounts of ferns on the way back to Glen Cairn. Delighted with their find, they happily scattered bouquets of greenery around the great hall.

With rational thinking restored and time at last to herself, Lily again began a letter to her mother.

Dear Mama…

Gnawing at the end of the quill pen, she thought

how best to explain Charlotte and her delay from the funeral. For whoever stayed longer than necessary at a funeral event?

A sharp rap at the door startled her. The possibility Edan stood on the opposite side filled her with dread—and a tiny tingle of delight. Tamping down the delight and restoring her composure, Lily called out as cheerfully as possible, "Come in!"

Charlotte poked her head round the door. Relief rolled over Lily like cooling rain on a sweltering summer's day in London. "Good even', sweet."

"The great hall is prepared," her sister reported with a satisfied smile.

"You've been a splendid help."

"And Maisie as well. Working together, we have struck up a fine friendship."

"Excellent."

"However, I am quite fatigued and will take supper in my chamber."

The work, as any work would, had taken its toll on Charlotte. Lily grinned, feeling a bit smug but persuaded her sister had taken the first step toward leaving her mollycoddled life behind. "I am rather weary myself, so I will join you."

"You will?"

"The Cameron brothers will be happy to dine by themselves tonight."

"Without being told how to use a knife?" Charlotte raised a skeptical brow.

Lily grinned. Now and again, her sister exhibited an amusing wit. "Exactly."

"And tomorrow during the gala, the laird will accept your proposal," Charlotte declared.

"Aye. I am certain of it." *Not at all.*

"He cannot keep you waiting much longer. T'would be too cruel."

"The laird has much on his mind. He would never be cruel, 'tis not in his nature. Go on with you now. I shall come to your chamber in a few moments."

Actually, Lily worried exceedingly about the laird's intentions. He seemed inclined toward her one moment but not the next. She only held a show of confidence for Charlotte's sake. With hope dwindling, she spent another restless night envisioning frightening scenarios of the many ways Edan might reject her proposal.

The day of the ceilidh dawned. Drowsy from lack of sleep, Lily felt cranky. Her time had just about run out for receiving an answer from Edan to her proposal. Pushing the fear of rejection out of her head, she spent the morning running about taking care of last-minute matters with Charlotte, Maisie, and Netta, who at last seemed to be warming to her.

Normal Highland weather had given way to a fine fall day with no rain in sight and just a nip of cool in the air. Lily gave thanks for the brisk day complete with a clear blue sky and bright sun. She could not have ordered more perfect ceilidh weather. The mouthwatering fragrance of mutton, fresh-baked shortbread, and mountains of home cooked dishes permeated the garden and great hall.

With the arrival of the first guests in the afternoon, Lily retreated to her chamber to change her gown and have Jane dress her hair. Soon laughter and music filled the air, drifting up to her chamber windows. Fiddles and drums and bagpipes played with Highland energy.

The sounds of joy encouraged Lily, gave her a sense of happiness.

By the time she returned to the party, the Cameron brothers were already in attendance. Angus danced with a laughing woman who flaunted bright red hair to match his own. Maisie joined Lily and Charlotte, identifying the guests as they arrived. "'Tis Pegeen Macalister who favors Angus," she said.

In Lily's opinion, Pegeen's abundance of curves and laughing eyes seemed right for Angus. Perhaps he had found his bride. She hoped he would ask the woman to dance.

She looked for Finn and found him in a corner sipping ale with a dark-haired beauty who smiled up at him with adoring eyes. The woman did not appear to be conversing with him, rather just listening. Lily hoped Finn's intelligence would not bore the beauty. Or the beauty would not bore Finn. He deserved an abundance of love and happiness. Hope filled Lily's heart.

Her gaze roamed swiftly around the hall. Those guests who had chosen to gather inside as dusk descended, closer to the music and dancing appeared happily engaged. But where was Edan?

Dancing.

He danced with one partner after another. Each partner brazenly flirted with the Laird of Glen Carin, laughing, and offering seductive smiles. After observing the sixth woman's efforts, not that she was counting, Lily turned away. A green-eyed monster had arisen within her. After consuming a filled goblet of ale, she closed her eyes and swayed to the music, dreaming of having the laird to herself alone.

"Ye have done well, Lilith."

His breath on her neck as he whispered in her ear sent delicious chills rolling down her spine. "Why do you always sneak up on me?" she asked without turning to face him.

"Because 'tis easy to do so." Edan stepped to her side.

"You are pleased with the ceilidh?"

"Aye, vera."

"I have done what you asked."

"Aye. Although, my brothers, well, ah, Angus in particular, could use more instruction in manners, no'?"

"I do not perform miracles. Besides, he looks happy enough. I think Angus will always be able to take care of himself very nicely."

"Like ye. And Charlotte. She appears to have settled."

"She has a friend in Maisie."

"What follows for ye?"

Follows? Certainly he must understand what follows is his agreement to an arranged marriage with her. Did he not understand or was he teasing? She refused to beg.

The pit of Lily's stomach burned as if on fire. Without an agreement? She decided to give the striking laird another opportunity. "I…I am uncertain."

Why did he remain silent?

"Uncertain? Lilith Munro?" Edan asked, giving her a sensual slide of a smile.

"I suppose Charlotte and I shall return to London," she answered with as much bravado as she could manage. Torn between loving the laird and killing him, she lifted her head in haughty royalty fashion.

Before Edan could respond, a thundering shout

echoed through Glen Carin's great hall. "Brodies! Brodies approach!"

"Run to yer chamber," Edan ordered. "Take Charlotte and dinna leave 'til I come for ye."

Edan and Finn started for the main door of the manor house, followed closely by Angus.

"Brodies!" called the watch once again. "Main entrance."

Musicians and guests raced in the opposite direction, heading for the garden to take refuge behind hedges and trees.

Pulse racing, heart pounding, Lily rushed to Charlotte and dragged her sister and Maisie to the corridor. Keeping close to the wall, she made for the back steps that led to the bedchambers. She stopped. From this vantage point, she could see what was happening in the hall, but Edan could not see her. Charlotte ran up the stairs out of harm's way with Maisie not far behind.

"Ye are no welcome here, Ranulf Brodie," Edan shouted angrily. "State yer business."

Sounds of warriors at the ready came from the entrance hall. Lily held her breath listening to the clanking of metal and the whoosh of swords and pistols being unsheathed.

"We come to yer ceilidh."

Lily recognized the voice as that of Ranulf, the Brodie clan leader who had accused her of trespassing on his property. A fearsome man. She pressed her body against the cold, damp wall, unabashedly eavesdropping. It could not hurt to stay for just a moment more.

"I repeat. Yer no' welcome here."

"We come in peace."

"What say ye?" Edan demanded.

"We've done fighting," Ranulf snapped in reply. "Brodie land is for sale."

Silence. Lily feared that in the profound stillness the men might hear her surprised gasp.

Edan broke the silence, speaking slowly, "Ye will sell yer land?"

"We fought the Brits and now our own Scot brathers. We canna war every day for land invaded by Blackface sheep."

"Ye ask me to buy yer land?" Edan's tone bordered on incredulous.

"Aye. Yer flush and if ye dinna buy our land the English will take it."

Upon hearing Brodie's dire prediction and understanding the truth of it, Lily felt no pride in her English blood.

"What will ye do?" Wariness laced Edan's question.

"We're bound for Nova Scotia," Ranulf responded gruffly.

"The new Scotland?" Angus questioned. From the odd sound of his voice, Lily understood that he too could not believe what he was hearing.

"Aye."

"How much do ye want for your land?" Finn asked quietly.

Brodie lowered his voice and mumbled something Lily could not hear. Of all times! No matter how hard she strained she could not hear.

Edan's reply however, echoed in the great manor and down the corridors. "Ha! Ye dream, Brodie. Where would I find what ye ask? 'Tis no gold in the Highlands."

"Yer sellin' yer cattle, go on and sell yer sheep too, for the lot of good they'll do ye."

"I'm no' selling my sheep."

"Then ye be the fool. If another English jimmy takes over Brodie land ye won't mind. Ye like the English…especially you like the Munro lass, no?"

"I canna pay yer price," Edan replied flatly.

"More's the pity," Brodie scoffed.

Lily's heart went out to Edan. If only she could help him. But she could not even help her sister. The sense of failure washed over her like a blanket of thick, wet mud.

"Be gone, Brodie," Edan ordered.

Lily felt the sting of tears as she listened to Edan order Brodie away. She knew the laird would like nothing more than to acquire Brodie's land. She could almost feel his disappointment. The grunts of the malcontent band of Brodies, as they mounted their horses to leave blended with the sounds of their bitterness and hatred.

To Lily's relief, the murmurings of the ceilidh guests grew louder as they returned to the hall. She'd feared the arrival of the Brodies might mean a disastrous end to the ceilidh. Gathering her courage, Lily entered the hall as soon as the bagpipe sounded. Angus stood in the middle of the great chamber playing his pipes and encouraging the resumption of the festivities. Lily hurried to Edan's side. He and Finn were deep in conversation. She placed a hand on the laird's arm. "What will you do?" Lily asked

"I dinna ken."

"Petition the king?" Finn asked. Clearly rather than a question, he offered a suggestion.

"Perhaps. I have thinking to do. Finn, help Lilith until the ceilidh's end."

"Aye." He looked down on Lily with a warm smile.

She would always feel safe with Finn, but when Edan left the hall, the sun left with him. The chamber lost its warmth and light. Wrapping her arms around her waist, Lily shivered.

The ceilidh continued with most of those in attendance having no idea what had happened between Edan and Ranulf. Declared a success by all, the Camerons' ceilidh lasted until the wee hours of the morning. Long after Charlotte had retired to her chamber.

After seeing the last gala guest leave and spending an hour of restless tossing in her bed, Lily realized she could not sleep. The laird had not responded to her request for an arranged marriage, even after he'd admitted she'd done well with the tasks he'd given her. Edan faced a conundrum. Jamie had not returned from London with the profits from the sale of the cattle. With little resources, if a choice was to be made, Edan would and should buy the Brodie land rather than take on a wife.

In the flickering candlelight of her chamber, Lily came to a decision. She and Charlotte must return to London as soon as possible. Throwing a thick wool wrap around her and snatching up a lantern, she quietly left her bedchamber. Making her way from the manor, she wished to stroll in the garden and enjoy the full Highland moon for the last time.

Braced for the chill, the only sounds she heard were the bleating of the sheep. And the insistent noise inside her head. She must admit her mistake and return to London. She might yet be able to negotiate with Lady Frances. Perhaps her mother would agree to sell Lily into marriage first. 'Twas now the only way she could save Charlotte's future.

Head down, she fought the tears of failure. Failure to help her sister, failure to find the Doonie Purse, failure to seduce the laird...and failure to control her emotions. She'd lost her heart. To the man she meant to marry. Deep in thought without a care to where her feet stepped, she suddenly slammed against a wall. A wall that was Edan's chest.

She gasped.

He frowned.

Slivers of silvery light from the full moon illuminated the small area. Several seconds of silence passed save for the plaintive hooting of an owl as she regarded him in shock and dismay. She could not have been more stunned if the Prince Regent had been waiting there.

Edan's frosty gaze bored straight through her. "What are ye doing in the garden at this time of night, Lilith?"

She pulled her shawl more tightly around her. "Ah, simply exploring."

"By moonlight?"

Lily shrugged. Her emotions threatened to overcome her, raw feelings, deep sadness. She feared speaking, frightened her tears might run over in the form of an endless river. "Aye."

His frown deepened as he looked her over in a

slow, questioning appraisal.

Yet again, she felt the heat of a blush on her cheeks and was grateful for the momentary lack of moonlight as a cloud slipped over the moon. "And so ye chose to relieve your curiosity in the middle of the night?" he pressed.

"I could not sleep," she admitted. "And apparently you could not sleep either."

"Nay."

"Or you are here to meet a lover who has not arrived yet? A woman from the ceilidh."

"A laird must dance with all the lasses. But I have no time for lovers."

"I see." *Which put a swift final end to Lily's dreams.*

"Do ye?"

"Perhaps Brodie made you an offer that has left you sleepless?"

He ran a hand through his hair disturbing the tie so that the dark strands fell to his shoulders in haphazard fashion. "Aye."

"Are you prepared to purchase his land?" she asked.

"If I do not acquire Brodies' land, the English will give it to one of their dukes or barons or the like," he grumbled. "The Clearances continue."

"The Clearances are unjust. I understand, Edan."

"Do ye now? The Brits clearing Scotland of the Scots."

The bitterness in his voice took Lily's breath away. "I do. 'Tis not right nor fair."

"The English have made certain that I do no' have the funds to buy Brodie's land."

"I'm sorry. Truly I am."

"I would rather buy Brodie land than simply take it."

"You would not just take the land. I have learned that much about you since Charlotte and I arrived without warning."

He chuckled for a moment. A dry, caustic sound. "Ah, but I would if I did no' ken the Brodie clan is victim too. Every Scot suffers from English greed."

"You will find a way to succeed. You always have," she said.

Edan reached out, pulling Lily against him. He lowered his mouth to hers in a bruising, burning kiss. A kiss that became soft and sweet, a kiss brushing her lips with such tenderness it roused a deep ache within her. A honey-thick weakness poured through her. The deep-down soul desire for Edan that she'd struggled against for a lifetime rose within Lily with heart throbbing force.

Pushing against the enticing Highlander's chest of steel, Lily angled her head and pulled away from his lips, from his engulfing grip.

"I canna get enough of ye, it seems. Ye calm my nerves, Lilith, ease my worries." He spoke in a deep husky tone. His indigo gaze was riveted on hers. "How do ye do that? Have ye cast a spell?"

Stunned, Lily swallowed hard. Silenced by a kiss. She could not remember a time when she'd heard Edan's voice thick with desire, or seen his eyes fired with burning passion. Unable to drag her gaze away, she trembled with her own longing, her own desire. "L…Lady Frances would have your…your head for that kiss."

A slow crooked smile stole across his lips. "Tell me that ye are no invoking the name of yer mother?"

"Ye…yes," she stuttered. "Yes I am."

"If truth be told, I fear ye tonight more than I fear yer dragon of a mother."

"Me?"

"Ye have returned to Glen Carin to secure an arranged marriage with me?"

Lily's heart skipped and jumped. Nervous. Anticipating. "Yes."

"But ye have rarely mentioned yer proposal again since first you made it."

"I have not wished to vex you or further embarrass myself." She lowered her eyes, the words catching in her throat. "I can see now that my proposal was wrong. English blood runs through my veins and you have often said you desire a strong Highland woman."

"As indeed ye have proved to be."

Uncertain whether she'd heard him correctly, Lily shook her head, blinking back tears.

"Why else have ye changed your mind?"

"Edan, you have not given me an answer. I have come to understand that you cannot or will not consider marriage with me. I refuse to beg you for an answer you cannot give."

"I suspect ye have already been promised to another," he said, hooking his finger beneath her chin and lifting her gaze to meet his. "Confess, Lilith. Ye have come to me oot of desperation. Lady Frances has arranged a marriage for you as well as Charlotte."

A simple lie would set her free from this interrogation, an interrogation breaking her heart. But it was a lie Lily did not doubt would soon become truth.

"Yes," she murmured. "Lady Frances has promised me to another."

"And ye meant to marry me in order to thwart her plan?"

Looking into his eyes, she felt her heart breaking. Pain shot through her chest. She hated her lie, but 'twas a lie to free them both from an unwanted arrangement. She loved Edan more than she would ever love another man. Suppressing the desire to throw her arms around him and never let him go, she quietly told him a truth. One truth. "Only thinking of an arranged marriage fills me with despair. But with you, a friend, I once believed such an arrangement...bearable."

"Bearable? Is that all ye think of me, bearable?" he roared. "I am bearable?"

"Nay," she whispered. "More than bearable. We, we share history."

"Of sorts." Edan's eyes took on a far-away look as he harrumphed. "I dinna ken why ye agreed to Lady Frances's terms."

"To save Charlotte from a worse position."

"Charlotte. Has it ever occurred to ye that she might be capable of saving herself?"

"No. My sister is fragile and such an innocent."

"Despite ye wishing to use me for marriage, I am agreeable. Yer proposal will benefit both of us."

He said yes! He'd agreed. Hadn't he?

Too late. A cold wave of disappointment flooded through Lily. Edan was willing to marry her without loving her, which she could no longer accept. "'Tis too late, Edan."

"Nay. What if I were to hold ye hostage? What if I were to send word to Lady Frances that ye shall never be leaving Glen Carin?"

What was he saying? What did he mean?

Lily took a deep, ragged breath. "Force cannot change my mind. You cannot hold me prisoner, and do not be thinking you will be turning my head and changing my mind with a wink and a smile."

"Nay," he said, with a wink and a smile.

Her teeth chattered. The heat from his kiss had given way to the frosty air of the night.

"Stay with me," he said softly, "even though I am only bearable."

Tears she could no longer hold back rolled down her cheeks. "Please do not make my parting more difficult."

Edan moved in, kissing her wet cheek, kissing each tear. "Dinna cry. Dinna cry. Stay with me."

"I cannot stay."

"I offer ye a better arrangement than any Lady Frances can make. Can ye no' see?" he demanded, with all the intensity of a warrior planning battle strategy. "I canna offer ye jewels and such, but a marriage between us would solve vera many problems. Ye would live in your childhood home, the home yer father built for ye. Charlotte will be safe. And living here in Glen Carin away from Lady Frances ye will be happy. I promise ye willna see much of yer husband. I agree to yer proposal. 'Tis why you returned. What has changed, Lilith? What has changed?"

The pressure of his hands on her arms grew tighter.

She fell in love. That is what changed. Lily had fallen deeply in love with him, love he could not return. And she could not say it. She could not speak of her love. More importantly, Lily could not become an extra burden on him with many challenges and limited funds.

"I have nothing to offer ye but promises, but if ye stay, Lilith, ye have my word that I will protect you always. Ye will never have anything to fear."

Lily's heart raced like a wild hare chased by Brodie hunters. She wanted his love. She needed his love.

"Ye will be a longtime friend in my bed," he insisted.

A longtime friend in his bed? Fresh tears gathered behind her eyes already blurred by those unshed.

"How many lads and lasses have ye known who entered a marriage of convenience without knowing each other?" he pressed. His dark brows descended into a somber frown. "Dinna ye see? We will go on well together just as ye believe, for we are old friends."

"I…I always thought to marry for love."

"Love? Och!" Edan jerked his head back as if he might have been struck. Releasing Lily from his grip, he gave a dismissive wave of his hand. "A lass's fancy."

"Nay—"

"Love never lasts," he declared gruffly, softening as he continued, "but friendships do. I have always considered ye a friend and I, I have always been fond of ye. But there are…things ye don't know about me."

Lily's lips trembled as she forced a smile. Even though she'd heard some hesitancy in his declaration, she chose to believe Edan's admission that he had always been fond of her. But fondness was not enough. Not now.

"In a short time, my fortunes will be restored," he added hastily. "Ye shall wear Paris gowns if ye like."

The image of walking the moors in a Paris gown

brought a smile to her lips despite feeling more flustered than she'd ever experienced. No. Flustered was too mild a term. Perhaps it was frustration rushing from her head to her toes. Or might it be disappointment? Shock.

Chaos griped Lily, her mind, body, and soul. "No, I do not require Paris gowns."

She required only one thing.

The tall, compelling laird of her heart studied Lily in such a penetrating manner; it seemed as if he might be reading her thoughts. Waiting for her answer, he had just promised everything a woman could ask for, but not the one thing she now had to have…his love.

She shook her head. "Lady Frances expects me to return to London shortly. I…I have obligations in the city."

"I can protect ye from Lady Frances. Charlotte has depended upon ye too long and too much," he grumbled. "'Tis past time for her to stand on her own."

"Perhaps you're right, but…but I cannot abandon her."

"What harm can befall her with Lady Frances at her side?"

"She is betrothed to marry a man three times her age, a known wifebeater."

"Damnation!" Edan rolled his eyes. "And what can ye do?"

"Persuade my mother the marriage cannot happen." If she could arrange for Lady Frances to enjoy a generous income, Lily felt certain her mother would cry off on Charlotte's marriage.

"As if Lady Frances will listen to ye," Edan grunted with a tight twist of his lips.

Lily despaired of winning this argument, especially since her heart begged to marry the man, while her mind screamed, *no, no, no*.

"I must go," she said. "I'm weary and, and you have given me much to think about."

"Why hesitate when in the end ye'll do the right thing. The sensible thing. Ye will marry me."

His lips turned up in a knowing half-smile of victory which caused Lily to bristle with sudden anger. She straightened her shoulders, regarding him as haughtily as royalty.

Edan's assumption of triumph was premature. She had come to him with only marriage on her mind but then her heart became involved. 'Twas a confusing turn of fate. For now, nothing would do but the laird's love.

"Good night, Edan." Head held high, she turned on her heel and marched away.

Chapter 9

His kiss. His kiss. His kiss.

Edan's kiss was all Lily could think of as she lay in her bed, overtired and unable to sleep. Her mind raced, returning again and again to the warmth of Edan's lips and her wanton response, the heat of her body, the hungry ache deep within for more than his kiss. More of what, she did not know. She only knew that when at last the aching within her eased she would still want Edan, still need him. Lily loved the Laird of Glen Carin, heart and soul. 'Twas as simple as that.

Edan needed a wife, but he did not love her, a fact neither simple nor acceptable any longer. If only she could stay as he'd asked. If she had more time to spend with him, perhaps he would learn to love her. But that was not to be. Lily had not the luxury of time to win the rugged laird's heart, even if she knew how. There were too many "if's" to overcome. Tears spilled down her cheeks. She had never in her life cried as much. Finally, she cried herself to sleep. It seemed the only way to remain within the warmth of Edan's embrace was to dream of him.

Lily woke with a start as a wide swath of bright sunlight streamed across her bed.

"Good morning, milady," Jane greeted her with a broad smile. "I feared you would have my head if I let you sleep the day away."

Rubbing her eyes, Lily scooted up in the bed. "What is the time?"

"'Tis going on ten o'clock. Are you feeling ill?"

"No. No." She shook her head as if she might shake out a veil of cobwebs. "I didn't hear the clock chime."

"I don't think the clock has chimed of late. Mayhap it has stopped."

"Poor Netta has too much to do. 'Tis impossible for her to accomplish everything in a day. Perhaps I can convince the laird to hire Maisie to help."

Jane's light brown curls bobbed as she nodded in agreement. "I brought you a cup of chocolate," she said, setting the porcelain cup on a bedside table.

"Thank you, but I must get dressed. There is much to do, and we must prepare to return to England as well."

Jane's brows shot up in undisguised surprise. "Return?"

"I am not certain when, but soon. Perhaps on the morrow. Please begin the packing."

Lily's young maid appeared saddened. "Yes, milady."

"We came to visit; we did not come to stay." Despite what she said, her maid knew very well why they had come to Glen Carin. Servants always knew the truth. Lily felt the heat of tears building behind her eyes. *Again?* She could not remember a time in her life she had shed so many tears.

Thirty minutes later, she stood before the mirror, her hair pulled back into an unbecoming knot at the top of her head, as near to being fashionable as she would come on this day. Thankfully, she did not look the less for wear. Only the light purple shadows beneath her eyes gave away her lack of sleep from the night before.

Knowing her sister was a late sleeper and a young woman who had danced the night away during the party, Lily knocked softly on Charlotte's door. "Charlotte? Are you awake?"

Charlotte's maid, Della, opened the door.

"Good morning," her sister yawned from the bed.

"At least you are awake and sitting up. I expect you are weary."

"I'm exhausted, but the ceilidh was the most fun I've had since we arrived at Glen Carin."

"'Tis well because we shall be leaving on the morrow."

"Leaving?"

Lily nodded. "Early tomorrow morning."

"No."

"No?"

"'Tis too soon, Lily." Inching her way down into the bed, Charlotte pulled up the covers. "I shall not be rested near enough."

"I cannot believe you are saying this. You wished to leave the day we arrived."

"True, but this morn I am happy. And exhausted from the ceilidh." Charlotte added a yawn for emphasis.

"But I am not. Neither exhausted nor happy."

"Oh, Lily. Sister dear." Charlotte's eyes grew moist as she regarded Lily with sympathy. "The laird turned down your proposal, did he not? He is the reason why you are in a bad temper. I am sorry indeed. He appeared to be more in favor of you of late. I—"

Lily interrupted briskly. "We will talk later after I break fast. In the meantime, get dressed. I shall have biscuits and chocolate sent up to you."

Bristling, Lily bolted, refusing to discuss her failure with Edan. Not with her sister or anyone else. In fact, she doubted ever recovering from the blow to her pride. If it were possible to retreat to her bed and pull the covers up over her head—she would. For months.

Leaving her sister's bedchamber, she eyed the Longcase clock in the corridor. Just as Jane suspected, the clock had stopped. She gave a sigh for Netta. The overworked housekeeper had so much to do she'd obviously neglected to wind the eight-day clock. But Lily could help with this much at least and feel she'd done something toward lightening the woman's work.

With a bit of a tug, Lily opened the bottom glass case. There were two weights, one to drive the pendulum and one to drive the striking element responsible for the chimes. Two keyholes were positioned on either side of the dial, to wind each one.

As she reached to pick up the keys lying on the base of the clock, she noticed another keyhole. She could not imagine what purpose it served, and when she tried the two winding keys in the extra keyhole, neither fit. Could it be? Wonder-struck, Lily clapped a hand over her mouth. Could one of the odd keys in her jewel box be the one to unlock this spare space?

Confident no one lurked in the corridor, Lily hurried to her chamber. After fetching the mysterious keys from her jewel box, she opened the door. Her heart pounded with apprehension as she peered up and down the corridor. Her hands shook. If caught, how could she explain delving into the Longcase clock? Swallowing hard and tamping down her anxiety, Lily tiptoed across the corridor to the clock.

Inhaling deeply, she silently counted to ten, warning herself not to be disappointed if the key did not fit. Slowly, she opened the glass door. Her hand shook so badly she dropped the key to the bottom. Scooping it up quickly, she slipped the key in the hole. The key fit.

Slowly, she turned the key in the lock. It did not move. Her mouth felt as dry as stale bread. Holding her breath, she applied more pressure and tried once again. This time…a small square opened. Her hand shook like a trembling old woman's as she reached down into the square space. Leather. She touched leather. Pulse racing with excitement, she withdrew a small dark leather pouch. She'd found it! The Doonie Purse! The Doonie Purse indeed existed!

Mother Have Mercy!

Lily's first instinct was to scream with joy. Her second was to dance down the corridor. But of course she could do none of those things, especially not knowing what the purse held. Tears streamed down her cheeks as she withdrew the pouch and loosened the drawstring. Tears of joy. She peered inside the pouch. Gold. Shiny gold chunks of all sizes winked up at her. She stifled the laughter of relief and utter exhilaration that bubbled up from deep within her.

Her heart swelled tightly against her chest, suddenly too large for its space, too filled with love for the father whose spirit touched her as the longcase clock chimed a new time. Standing alone in the dim, damp corridor, she gave silent thanks. Lily now possessed the means to save Charlotte from the dreaded marriage…or for Edan to purchase the Brodie land.

Clutching the purse close to her, Lily quickly retreated to her chamber. Once behind the closed door, she spilled the contents of the purse on her bed and viewed the promise of her father. 'Twas not a fairy tale or a fantasy. The Doonie Purse indeed existed, its contents lovingly put aside by her da, contents meant to rescue Charlotte and her when Lady Frances failed.

Gathering up the contents, she poured the gold nuggets back into the velvet pouch and tucked the treasure beneath her mattress, feeling secure in what she must do.

First, in order to keep her secret, she needed to cover her tracks. Lily had not only neglected to close the Longcase Clock case, she hadn't reset the clock as she'd intended. Returning to the corridor, she corrected her missteps.

Releasing a deep sigh, she straightened, closed the case, and turned—into Edan.

"What are ye doing, lass?"

Disconcerted by his silent appearance, she sputtered, "the clock...the clock had stopped and required winding."

"Yer jumpy. Did I give you a fright?"

"I...I didn't hear you."

"Well, I dinna sneak upon ye."

"Aye, you did." She lowered her gaze. "You're not wearing boots."

He chuckled. "My boots are being cleaned."

"Which is why I did not hear you."

He chuckled again.

"Do you believe in the Doonies?" she asked in a nonchalant tone.

"Does not every Scot?"

"My da spoke of a Doonie purse to me. He loved his Doonie stories as much as this clock."

140

****

The clock began to chime. Ten chimes. The music of the chimes echoed through the corridor. Edan watched the glow of love on Lilith's face as she listened. 'Twas music to her ears, he knew.

He recognized the importance of the Longcase to Lilith. He knew the history and why Rob Munro commissioned the clock from the prominent British clockmaker, Thomas Tompion. Years before, Munro had proudly confided in Edan that importing the clock for his bride had been a labor of love. Rob always referred to his wife as his bride. If only Lady Frances had been worthy of such devotion.

"Come, Lilith." He took her hand, leading her away from the clock and downstairs to the dining hall where they would break fast.

The delicious, spicy cinnamon taste of her still lingered on his lips. Each day it seemed he discovered something new and fascinating about the lass he'd hardly thought about after she'd left the Highlands. Except in a bothersome way. He remembered well the times Lilith had plagued him. Now he could hardly think about anything else but how Lilith Munro pleased him. It was as if she'd cast a spell on him. Her shining, meadow-green eyes and her enchanting smile never left his mind.

After their early morning meeting in the garden, he'd gone to his bed with an ache so painful he found it difficult to sleep. He could think of nothing but having Lilith in his bed, kissing her, holding her as he'd done on the terrace. He must have her, night after night, holding her through the night, loving her until dawn's first light. 'Twas no longer a decision to make, 'twas a fact to act upon.

Working without respite to restore his land, he'd gone too long without a woman. Enough reason, he suspected, for wanting the beautiful willowy lass more than he'd ever wanted any female. She'd taken him by surprise, emerging from the manor in the middle of the night. He'd returned the surprise by pulling her into his arms and kissing her fiercely—a move that had left him shaken to his core.

He pulled her along, thinking. Thinking.

But what of her? Lilith had appeared untouched. She'd refused to marry him. While not an arrogant man by nature, in the past his kisses had caused many a maiden to swoon. Had he lost his touch? Och, no! Impossible.

With Lily, his kiss had gone deeper, stirred by inescapable desire. 'Twas like stoking low burning embers that suddenly burst into flame. The fire consumed him. She meant more to him than a quick kiss in a dark corner.

Edan could understand Lilith wishing to reacquaint herself with Glen Carin, but not in the middle of the night. She too must have been walking off her troubled thoughts, just as he had. After several disquieting hours, he had come to an understanding. He was not his father. If ever he had ever been. Lilith had made him a better man. She had shown him possibility, the way to a gratifying future.

And now she rejected him? Suspicion niggled at the back of Edan's mind. Why had she changed her mind about a marriage of convenience? There was not a maiden in the Highlands who would not marry him in less time than it took to light a candle.

The great hall door slammed shut, obliterating all thoughts of the sorceress Munro.

Edan started, as did Lily who froze in her tracks.

He worried that Brodie had returned without warning. Scenario after scenario tumbled through his mind. He squeezed Lilith's hand as he attempted to solve the threat Brodie posed. Edan swore he would never allow any harm to come to the lass at his side. Ever.

Time seemed to have come to a stop. Not a sound could be heard. The savory scents of the breakfast meal drifted up the stairs. Salmon and fresh-baked scones.

Lily's stomach growled. She was hungry and yet did not move. She stood still as a statue. In wait. For what? She barely breathed.

"What the hey?" Angus's voice thundered.

"I'm home, brather!"

Jamie!

Lily recognized Jamie's voice and a rush of relief swept through her. She pulled her hand from the warmth of Edan's. The youngest Cameron had arrived home at last.

"Jamie?" Edan's voice rumbled in a deep, not so welcoming tone. He rushed down the stairs to the corridor where his brothers stood. Lily followed.

"Am I in time to break fast?" Jamie asked with a grin.

Angus slapped the young man on the back. "Aye."

"Enough, Gus. Ye'll knock me over."

"Where have ye been, Jamie Cameron?" Edan demanded, much to Lily's dismay. She'd hoped the laird would save his anger for another day.

"Doing yer bidding, dear brather." Jamie bowed

from the waist in mock respect. "My thanks for the warm welcome home."

"We expected ye weeks ago. Did ye run into trouble?"

"No more than usual. Dinna growl at me. I carry the funds from the cattle sale in London. Better profits than ever before."

Lily hurried to Edan's side. "Jamie, 'tis lovely to see you," she said with a slight dip of her head.

Jamie flashed another of his heart-melting grins. "Lilith Munro, 'tis a relief to see ye safely at home in Glen Carin."

"You may not feel that way after I have a word with you."

He regarded Lily with the warmth and charm which rendered many a young woman speechless. "Nay. No matter what or why, I shall always hold you in the greatest esteem."

"As well ye should," Edan declared darkly.

Jamie glanced to the stairs, to the dining chamber and back to the stairs. "And where might Charlotte be? Does she wait in the dining chamber?"

Undoubtedly, Lily thought, Jamie was the most instantly endearing of the Cameron brothers. Nothing said or done seemed ever to faze the man. But how did he know Charlotte had come with her? "My sister is in her bedchamber."

"Come," Edan ordered. "Have tea and spin us yer tall tale."

"Aye," Jamie agreed readily, pausing at the entrance to the dining chamber. "But Charlotte must join us."

"Why?" Lily asked, both curious and startled.

His grin grew wider, and his dark eyes sparkled with mischief. "I have missed yer sister and I bring good news to share."

"Missed her?" The look in Jamie's eyes alarmed Lily. What was the boy up to? She scanned the chamber until she found Netta. "Please ask Charlotte to join us at once."

Charlotte appeared quickly. Out of character, quickly, thought Lily. She along with Edan and Angus had just sat down to the table. Without a glance to the others, Charlotte dashed to Jamie's side. Standing at the buffet, he quickly set his plate aside and took both her hands in his. "Charlotte, me love."

"Jamie." With eyes burning bright, she turned to Lily. "Before we left London, Jamie and I agreed to meet at Glen Carin."

"Yer love?" Edan frowned, cutting his youngest brother a look that would terrify most men.

"Your love?" Lily repeated with a squeak jumping to her feet.

Charlotte cast her most brilliant smile, first to Edan and then to Lily. "We wish to marry. We wished to be married here in Jamie's home. Glen Carin."

Her smile, her soft explanation served to quiet the hall.

Stunned and without words, for one of the very few times in her life, Lily could only stare at her sister. But just for a moment. "You wish to wed Jamie?" she questioned, completely perplexed and quite certain she did not understand. "You are in love? You have discussed—"

"Yes!" Charlotte's exclamation was followed by a giggle. "When this handsome Scotsman appeared in

Hyde Park, he stole my heart. I could not allow Mama to marry me to that old scoundrel Whetfield when each day I fell more in love with Jamie." She paused to give a lovelorn sigh. "Begging your pardon, Lily, but I took control of my destiny."

Destiny or desperation? Lily feared Charlotte might wish to marry Jamie for the wrong reason. "But I told you I would help you—"

"No need," her blissful sister interrupted. "You have helped me enough. We will marry now that Jamie is home, and I will face Mama. 'Tis time for me to stand or fall on my own."

Animated, ever animated, Charlotte appeared radiant. Her joy spilled over into the hall and the family and servants gathered there. Hesitant smiles, but smiles nonetheless, began to appear on the lips of the hardened Highlanders and the sour-faced housekeeper.

Although Lily would never have imagined such a match, Charlotte had never looked happier, or lovelier. The heightened pink of her cheeks and lips complimented her blonde curls and blue eyes even more. Charlotte's gaze returned again and again to the man who was to be her husband, the youngest Cameron. Jamie, in turn, never looked away from Charlotte.

Astonished, Lily slowly realized her sister's wish to marry Jamie truly was for love alone.

"I have loved Charlotte from the minute I set eyes on her that first day riding in the park," Jamie explained, turning to Lily. "Eventually, she confided in me, telling me that ye planned a secret trip to Glen Carin to propose an arranged marriage with Edan. 'Twas then I knew how to make the escape from Lady

Frances. I asked Charlotte to marry me at Glen Carin. To wait for me in my Highland home."

"I said yes," Charlotte added unnecessarily.

"But you did not tell me," Lily protested. "Instead, you made it appear as if you were miserable. You told me you wished to go home, back to London."

"I did not want you to think I had taken advantage of your scheme for my own purposes."

Although she absolutely had.

Worse, Lily's reason for their journey, to make an arranged marriage with Edan no longer served a purpose. Charlotte did not need Lily to save her from a dangerous marriage. The laird had made it clear he did not love Lily. But his love had become important to her, as necessary as breathing. Without Edan's love she could not marry him. She could not remain at Glen Carin. It was impossible. Like a twig, snapped and tossed aside, her heart shattered.

Edan's grin left no doubt of his pleasure. Making his way to Charlotte's side, he bussed her on the forehead and swept the laughing young woman into his arms. "Charlotte. Ye will be our most bonnie sister from this day, forever under the protection of all the Camerons. We shall protect you from Lady Frances or any who might wish you harm."

Slipping out of his arms, Charlotte bobbed a curtsey. "Thank you, Your Grace."

Chuckling, Edan called out, "Netta! Prepare a feast! We shall celebrate Jamie and Lady Charlotte's engagement this evening."

Angus took Charlotte in his arms, bestowing a great bear hug before releasing her with a promise, "I'll be piping for ye tonight."

Tamping down a myriad of questions, Lily circled an arm around Charlotte's shoulder and scooted her away from the brothers. "You had me fooled. Until this morning when you told me you were not ready to leave."

Charlotte shot Lily a coy smile before turning to bat her eyelashes at Jamie. He responded with a grin only a man deeply in love could give.

Lily felt a stab of what might have been jealousy for Charlotte and Jamie. She looked to Edan, whose smile had disappeared. Clearing his throat, he threw Lily an agitated frown.

Why he would be irritated with her? Lily did not understand, but she quickly came to the conclusion that she and Charlotte would be better off by themselves until all questions were answered to her satisfaction. "Come, Charlotte, let us retire to my chamber."

"And you, Jamie," Edan folded his arms across his chest in masterful fashion. "Ye have some explaining to do."

"As do you," Lily whispered to Charlotte.

Chapter 10

Fuming, eye twitching relentlessly, Lily all but pushed Charlotte through the door to her bedchamber. "Why did you not confide in me about Jamie?"

Her sister offered an apologetic smile. "I feared I might be dreaming. Or that perhaps he did not truly mean to marry me. Or even worse, that while we were separated Jamie would forget he ever loved me. I did not wish to feel the fool."

Lily nodded. She knew how it felt to feel the fool. Her journey to seek an arranged marriage with an old…friend, had indeed been a fool's mission. She forced a sympathetic smile. "I…I understand, sweet." She also understood too well the uncertainty of love. "I do."

Charlotte spread her arms and twirled round in place, skirts billowing. "You cannot imagine how lovely I feel!" she gushed. "Jamie loves me! We shall be married in days! Perhaps on the morrow." Coming to an abrupt halt, suddenly serious, she snatched Lily's hand and held it tightly. "You need not worry. You shall live with us here in Glen Carin. Edan will soon realize his mistake and come to love you."

Lily gasped. She could not reconcile the change in Charlotte. Who was this young woman twirling about the chamber vowing to take care of her? "I, I do not know what to say," she stammered. "Truly, I do not."

"You need not say a thing. Mama cannot make us return to London now, you know." Beaming, Charlotte flopped on Lily's bed.

"No, you will be safe with Jamie." Lily had expected, as did all who knew Jamie, that with his roving eye and winning personality he would be the last of the Cameron brothers to marry. But she knew Jamie was as honorable a man as his brothers and was certain he would be a good and kind husband to Charlotte. Still, she could not deny her shock. "Tell me, how did you form an attachment so quickly? Why did I not see?"

"Jamie and I met in the park on the first lovely day in spring when I walked with you. And many days afterwards," she added with a sly smile. "Unbeknownst to you and mama, I stole away to Hyde Park to meet Jamie at every opportunity. Almost every day. 'Twas like a spark between us that cannot be explained. We walked, we talked, and we fell in love. He is the most handsome man ever!" she insisted. "And the most intelligent of men."

No. In Lily's opinion Edan was far more handsome and more intelligent than any of the other Cameron brothers. Comparing Edan to Jamie was akin to comparing a striking giant with a pale mortal. Edan exuded strength and manliness. Jamie radiated charm and foppish style. Unwilling to put a damper on her sister's happiness, Lily agreed with a nod of her head. "Sweet, you gave me the impression that you did not like the Highlands. I thought you could not be happy here."

"Jamie's home is my home. I can be happy anywhere and wherever he is. Besides, Scot blood runs through my veins the same as yours." The bride-to-be jumped off the bed and darted to the door. "We shall discuss wedding plans later."

"Wait! What of Mama? Does she know what you've done? She will be furious."

"Several days ago, I sent a message explaining I meant to wed Jamie Cameron and we would be residing in his ancestral Highland home."

"Oh, no!"

"I have said many prayers since. Do not worry."

"She knows where you are! Where *we* are!" *Oh. No.*

"Unless the message never reached London," Charlotte suggested with a hopeful lilt to her voice.

"She'll come after you! After us!"

"Jamie promised me that we will deal with that eventuality if it should happen. But weeks ago while we were still in London, he convinced me 'tis far better not to worry about something that may never happen."

"Oh, it will happen, Charlotte. Mama will happen."

"She does not like to travel."

Lily clapped her hands to her cheeks. "Mother Have Mercy!"

"Our Mama? Mercy? I do not expect so, and I am prepared for a bit of shrieking and tears," Charlotte informed Lily. "Jamie and I have discussed the repercussions."

"And is Jamie prepared to support Lady Frances in the style she's become accustomed?"

"He means to speak to the laird about arranging Mama's future."

"Edan?" Lily sank to the edge of her bed. "Dear God."

He sister's brows gathered in a questioning frown. "Will he not help us?"

"The laird has many responsibilities as it is, Charlotte."

Her sister gave a resigned smile. "'Tis a laird's lot in life. Did you not know?"

"I…I…I think we must give more thought to this situation—and to Mama."

Charlotte's blue eyes twinkled with happiness as she nodded her agreement. "Later. I cannot think of Mama now. Perhaps after Jamie and I walk in the garden. I have missed him so."

As soon as the bedchamber door closed behind her bubbling sister, Lily sank to her bed.

'Twas like a spark between us that cannot be explained.

Love was the spark, Lily knew, no explanation required. She'd felt it herself.

Her head spun with disturbing possibilities, all of them to do with Lady Frances's reaction to Charlotte's adventure—and hers.

Several minutes later, still a bit dazed, Lily roused herself to answer the quiet rap on her door. She assumed Charlotte had returned with some forgotten news of major importance.

But it was not her sister who stalked into the room slamming the door closed behind him.

"What are we going to do aboot this?" Edan clasped his hands behind his back, his eyes flashed with anger and his brow was drawn deep in anger.

"I…I don't know if there is anything we can do."

The obviously disturbed Laird of Glen Carin turned on Lily, lashing out. "Do ye ken what that foolish brother of mine expects of me? He expects me to support Lady Frances into her dotage."

Into her dotage? That might prove to be many, many years. Lily had firsthand knowledge on how well her mother took care of herself. She released a heavy sigh. "I fear Jamie is just as naïve as Charlotte," she said. "They are quite a pair."

"'Tis no excuse," Edan grumbled.

Lily had the feeling he would spit fire if it were possible; such was the laird's anger. But understanding Edan's anger wasn't directed at her, Lily softened her voice in an attempt to calm him. "Jamie is in love…as is Charlotte."

"Love!" He rolled his eyes and began to pace the room, circling Lily as he thundered aloud his thoughts. "Och! 'Tis well for them. I have no objection. But how am I to buy more sheep, purchase the Brodie land, plant barley, and support the habits of yer spendthrift mother?"

"We shall—"

"Lady Frances, a shr…woman who has never disguised her dislike of Highlanders in general and Camerons in particular. Canna purchase all this with love, Lilith?"

"No. You cannot be expected to take so much on yourself—"

"Dinna forget I am the Laird of Glen Carin, the chief of what is left of the Cameron Clan. I am responsible for every soul beneath my roof and Cameron Castle's as well. I have never shirked my duties and I never will."

"It is possible Lady Frances may come after Charlotte, take her back to England, and have the marriage annulled," Lily theorized, feeling the cold hands of misery creeping over her.

"Would she have the marriage annulled if yer sister was with child?" he barked.

Lily opened her mouth to reply, but nothing emerged. She hadn't thought of such an eventuality. But even now, Charlotte could be with child. With that numbing realization, Lily's entire body trembled. Steadying herself, she took a deep breath and spoke softly, "Do you know something I do not?"

"Nay," he replied curtly. "Nay. I dinna mean to cast unjust aspersions on Charlotte. But my brother is clever, and apparently besotted, which can make any man mindless."

"Let us take one trouble at a time." Lily lowered her voice in an attempt to restore calm to the conversation—and herself. "Tonight, let us celebrate the union of your brother and my sister. With a bit of good fortune, they will be wed on the morrow before my mother can do anything to disrupt their marriage. Perhaps we can see them pledged in a handfasting if—"

"Och!" Edan interrupted. Talking aloud, but seemingly to himself, he resumed pacing around Lily as if she were the hub of a wheel. "We are the Camerons of Glen Carin. My brother and Charlotte shall be wed properly."

"I fear where my Mama is concerned, time is of the essence, Edan."

"Aye, aye," he agreed swiping a hand through his hair. "I shall never be able to support Lady Frances's extravagances."

"I shall tend to my mother. Purchase the sheep as you planned."

"And let the land go? 'Tis a rare opportunity, and with the Prince Regent's favor, he might allow me to purchase the Brodie property. I intend to petition him."

"Sadly, for the present perhaps you should forget Brodie's land," Lily suggested. She had no idea the price of sheep or land. She might help if she possessed more information and if Edan could swallow his pride.

"If I let go the Brodie land, the Brits will pass it to another Brit," Edan grumbled. "I canna let any more Scot land fall to the British."

With a puff of exasperation, Lily gazed upwards, keeping her voice even. "All Brits are not so terrible."

Evidently chastened, Edan lowered his voice, "Ye are no' terrible, Lilith, 'tis the prince and his cohorts. He gave me my land for my service against the French. My own land. He allowed me to keep Cameron land…as a gift. As mad an idea it might be, I believe he would also allow me to appropriate Brodie's land if I petition quickly."

"All right, then. Perhaps you should not worry about sheep or Lady Frances at present and instead concentrate on acquiring Brodie's land. There are always compromises to be made. You shall solve these puzzles. You shall prevail."

His gaze fixed on Lily, filled with wonder and something else she could not quite define. He spoke softly. "You have more faith in me than I do."

"Only think, Edan. Think about other times when you were mired in dark circumstances and unexpectedly found light. Life has a way of working out for the best," she said. With all her heart Lily wished to calm and comfort the laird. "If Mama should be vexed, I shall tend to her." *To be certain, Mama would be vexed. More than vexed.*

The laird angled his head casting a doubtful expression Lily's way.

"Do not fret about my mother," she coaxed with a smile.

"Aye. But ye canna allow Lady Frances to have her way with ye. Ye came here to marry me—and you shall." Edan shook his head, unleashing and disheveling his thick dark waves of hair. Swiping a hand through the mass in a worried gesture, he stalked to the door. "I am vera sorry for disturbing ye. I should not have burdened you with my thoughts."

"A man requires a sounding board on occasion."

He reached out to open the door but looked back at her. His gaze cut to hers and he shot her a wry smile. "Ye, more than my brothers, have become my voice of reason."

Returning his smile, Lily gave a quick courtsey. "I am glad to be of help."

As soon as the door closed behind him, Lily took a deep breath, the first she'd taken since hearing Jamie's voice. She may have calmed Edan, but her own belly rolled in continuous, upsetting somersaults.

"You came here to marry me, and you shall." Had he truly just made such a declaration? Yes, he had.

Tears burned behind Lily's eyes, awaiting release. Marriage to Edan had taken on a new dimension. Since she no longer had Charlotte's future to consider, a marriage of convenience with Edan held no promise. 'Twas not nearly enough. Lily had fallen in love with the proud Scot. Indubitably in love. She no longer harbored a child's infatuation. The woman she had become required more; she required his love in return.

Hours later, time which passed way too swiftly, Lily prepared for the evening celebration of Jamie and Charlotte's love and imminent marriage. "Jane, please unpack my blue gown. I should like to wear it this evening."

"Should I unpack all your gowns, then?" asked Jane, barely concealing her excitement.

"No. My plans have not changed. You and I shall leave on the morrow for London."

Lily meant to bargain with the devil. Meaning her mother. If Lady Frances agreed not to meddle in the marriage of Charlotte and Jamie; Lily would agree to any marriage her mother arranged for her. Bowing to Lady Frances wishes would save Edan from supporting the luxurious life to which her mother was accustomed, and Charlotte would be free to live happily with Jamie in Glen Carin.

Lily might not be able to save the world, but she possessed the means to save the people she loved from unhappiness or a life of misery. Besides, if she could not be married to the love of her life, Lily did not care who she married—although she would prefer a husband who did not beat her.

After she returned to London, she wished Edan to remember her as the woman who loved him unconditionally and who left her heart with him in the Highlands. Not as the woman he nearly wed in a marriage of convenience.

Jane helped her don the only gown she had not yet worn in Glen Carin. The beautiful blue silk dress was the color of a soft summer sky. Delicate ivory lace trimmed the puffed sleeves, the high waist, and hem. Lily had Jane remove the lace at her neckline so that a hint of décolletage beckoned the eye. After giving her hair a final touch with the help of her treasured lady's maid, Lily stood ready to celebrate.

The lilting music of a lone bagpipe and the scent of roast lamb filled the great dining hall. The Cameron brothers were dressed in their finest clan kilts, tartans of deep red and forest green plaid. A finer looking group of men could not be found in the Highlands or in London for that matter, Edan being the most splendid among them. The laird caused Lily's heart to beat faster and her body to grow warm with only a glance. He stirred a growing need within her. A restlessness. Even as Lily lost herself in silent admiration, the magnificent Scot smiled at her across the room. Breaking off his conversation with Jamie, he started toward her, a half-smile dancing on his lips.

"Ye look vera bonnie, Lilith."

"And you, Laird of Glen Carin, Viscount of Bennington are quite dashing dressed in your plaid."

Edan chuckled as he dipped his head in what appeared to be a sheepish acknowledgement. "I appreciate ye hearing me out earlier. Before ye came back to Glen Carin, I had no need to share my thoughts. I dinna mean to upset ye."

"You did not upset me. As I cautioned, in my experience, troubling problems have a way of working out," she replied, wishing she could believe her own words of comfort. Hoping that after she'd left Glen Carin her plans would ensure the happiest life for Edan, Charlotte, and Jamie.

"Jamie assures me he has given up his irresponsible ways for the love of Charlotte. He promises to work with Angus, Finn, and me to restore

Glen Carin and Cameron Castle."

"You are fortunate to have a strong family willing to help you."

He nodded, lifting his gaze to look over her shoulder. "Ah, here is yer sister."

Lily turned to greet Charlotte. Dressed in pale lavender, her sister had never looked lovelier, causing Lily's heart to swell with pride. Charlotte aimed her brightest smile at Edan as she dipped into a deep curtsey. "My laird, you are a good kind man, and I shall be so honored to call you brother."

"Och! Ye are a keen-witted woman, as well as bonnie."

"I am very like my sister," Charlotte said.

Edan's brows shot up.

Laughing, Charlotte turned away, rushing to Jamie's side.

As usual for supper, Lily was seated to Edan's right, as she had been since their arrival. Her position as unofficial lady of the house never bothered her when alone, but with her sister seated at the same table for the first time, she squirmed, wondering what Charlotte would think. She hadn't long to wait before finding out.

Charlotte leaned closer and lowered her voice to the barest whisper, "The laird is so handsome, and you appear comfortable with him. Why return to London? If you can persuade Edan to marry you, we will be more than blood sisters. We shall be sisters in as many ways as possible. Just think! We shall be together forever! Do not give up on the laird, Lily."

But she already had given up on Edan. "Charlotte, sweet, my time here has come to an end. If I return quickly, perhaps I might stop Mama from coming after you."

Charlotte gave a toss of her head, whispering urgently, "Jamie gives me new strength. Mama may come after me, but I will not bend to her will ever again. And neither should you. Though I dislike saying so, she does not appreciate you."

"Lady Frances's lack of appreciation is beside the point."

"Anyone can see that almost overnight you have become more Cameron than Munro. The success of the ceilidh attests to the fact. The London Lily is gone. Edan obviously fancies the Highland Lily." One corner of Charlotte's mouth slid upward. "He cannot take his eyes off you."

Lily shook off her sister's sly grin. "You are a romantic, living on a cloud with Jamie."

"And you are the most remarkable woman any man could hope to marry."

"You are definitely partial, dear sister." But glancing from the corner of her eye, she caught Edan's gaze on her, powerful and yet plaintive. Lily straightened. "Charlotte, before I left London, I made an arrangement with Lady Frances that I must honor."

"Balderdash."

Her sister's bold comment rocked Lily back on her heels. *Did she say balderdash?* "What did you say?"

Charlotte grinned. "Balderdash."

Yes, she'd said Balderdash! Lily forced a patient smile. "Please mind your tongue and your manners. Must I remind you the Cameron brothers are attempting to learn the good graces of the ton."

"I shall say no more," she promised with a coy smile. A smile that unduly disturbed Lily.

Marked by mouthwatering aromas, the evening feast proved to be a merry event with many toasts of ale—Slainte!—and everyone on their best behavior. Goblets of fine Scotch whisky and ale were raised, filled, and refilled. Steaming dishes of lamb and tatties, haddock and kale were served along with nettle and venison. The savory dishes filling the table were followed at the end by gingerbread and Clootie dumpling.

The Cameron brothers did not sit for brandy and cigars after dinner as was the English custom. Following the meal, Jamie announced dancing in the parlor.

Dancing was the last thing Lily wished to do. Her conversation with Charlotte had disturbed her, and all she wished for was to escape to her bedchamber. Had the London Lily truly been lost?

"I ate too much," Angus complained.

"A dance or two will do ye well," Jamie replied.

Evidently unexcited about the prospect of dancing, Finn pointed out in a weary tone, "We are short of dance partners."

"Brathers, 'tis happy I am to learn that ye now dance," the bridegroom responded with a grin.

Finn gave Jamie a pained smile. "Lilith has been teaching us. 'Tis necessary to dance like kings when we attend the Edinburgh and London parties. Soon the Cameron brothers will be whisking the beautiful aristocratic lassies aboot the dance floor."

"Well, I wish to dance with each of you…starting with my husband-to-be, of course," Charlotte chirped.

The group followed Jamie and Charlotte into the parlor. To Lily's surprise, the carpet had been rolled up and two musicians, one at the pianoforte and one with a fiddle, waited to play. In his effort to give his bride-to-be a festive celebration, Jamie had been a busy man.

Mixed emotions warred within Lily. One moment her heart raced with happiness and in the next, the knot in her stomach tightened. She would miss Edan dreadfully and now Charlotte as well.

Her free-spirited sister had solved her own arranged marriage problem and no longer required help from Lily. But Edan, the laird, was another matter. Lily could best serve him by keeping Lady Frances at bay. She had no choice but to return to London quickly. Perhaps, she might even be able to arrange a marriage for her mother.

The laird stood across the room from her, watching the young couple dance. With his arms folded across his massive chest, he appeared the formidable laird he was, head of his clan, loved and respected by his family. His indigo gaze fixed on the joyous young couple. From where Lily stood, the jagged scar on his cheek seemed to disappear within the sun-leathered hue of his skin. She found it difficult to look away from the man she'd adored from an early age. In particular, Edan's muscular physique and remarkable eyes kept her enraptured.

She allowed a small smile when she noticed his left foot tapping to the beat of the music. Transfixed, she watched as he approached her, never taking her gaze from his. She felt the warmth of his smile; held her breath in anticipation as he held out his hand.

She placed her hand in his and immediately felt the tingle of a thousand warm pins and needles shooting through her. She stood, greeting him with a soft smile.

Her pulse quickened with strange excitement as he pulled her into his arms. Engulfed in the heat of his nearness, the strong yet tender touch of his hand on her back, she gave herself up to the magical spell of the moment—feeling loved. For although he had not said it, his loved filled and swelled her heart to near bursting. For one moment in time. A love, she'd only dared dream.

'Twas a fleeting spell she did not wish to break with conversation, and yet a conversation was needed.

"Best ye forget returning to London," he murmured, softly in her ear. "Now that yer sister will be married to Jamie in a matter of days, there is no reason for ye to leave the Highlands."

"Returning will satisfy my mother. She will not chase after Charlotte if I return. I must do what is right." Angling her head, she drew a strengthening breath and looked deeply into his eyes. "But what of you, Edan? Will you miss me?"

"What do ye think?"

"I think I would like to know how you feel."

"Och!" He threw back his head and rolled his eyes.

Amused? He felt both amused and vexed by her simple question?

With a swift wag of her head, Lily turned quickly to hide the tears. Suddenly chilled to the bone and with her belly burning as if she'd sipped hemlock, she hurried from the room. Of course he did not love her! He regarded her as little more than a servant, a woman to teach his brothers good manners. Edan had reduced Lily to a Sassenach who could arrange a ceilidh and win the hearts of the Highlanders for the Cameron Clan.

Holding her skirts, she dashed up the stairs. In the

corridor she heard Edan behind her, his giant steps echoing in the hall. Heart pounding, almost out of breath, Lily quickened her pace. To no avail. The compelling laird caught up with her just as she reached her bedchamber. As her hand reached for the latch, Edan seized her forearm, and in one smooth as silk motion, spun her around, pulled her against his body, and brought his mouth down on hers.

Lily felt as if she was drowning, lightheaded and spinning out of control, hot waves of desire swept over her. He smelled of soap and leather and man. His lips tasted of wine, as hers willingly parted beneath his hungry mouth. The man who ruled the Cameron clan also ruled her heart. Lily could not deny that a youngster's adoration had blossomed into a woman's devotion. His kisses, first tender and then in turn bruising, rendered her incapable of reason, or the will to tear out of his arms.

And just when Lily thought she might burst into flame, Edan grasped her shoulders and set her firmly back from him. His gaze collided with hers. "Do ye ken how I feel now?"

Chapter 11

"I…I…" Before Lily could finish a thought, let alone a sentence, Edan gave a curt nod and strode away, back to the festivities. The brawny laird walked away without looking back. He left her totally unfit for further socializing. He'd left her with a burning need. Unfulfilled.

Up until now, weak in the knees had only been an expression Lily had heard. At the moment, she felt so weak in the knees she wondered if she would be able to open the door before she collapsed on her bed. Wishing he was with her. Wishing he might say the words she longed to hear. Lust was one thing, love another. She felt the lust as much as Edan, but she felt so much more, needed so much more from him.

Lily moved slowly, one unsteady foot in front of the other. She managed to take refuge in her chamber and pull the bell rope for her maid. Jane appeared quickly and sounded hopeful when she asked. "Should I unpack, milady?"

Lily shook her head. She knew the servants were buzzing like bees. Rumors and conjectures concerning the activities in Glen Carin abounded. Two English sisters had arrived at the Glen Carin manor and turned the household upside down. "No." Lily shook her head vehemently. "We must return. I gave my word to Lady Frances we would return."

A somber-faced Jane helped Lily into a simple muslin embroidered night shift before leaving her. Lying in bed, staring up at the ceiling, Lily felt doomed. She dreaded returning to London. But in doing so she could prevent Lady Frances from coming to Glen Carin and tearing Charlotte away from the first true happiness she'd known. A cloak of sadness deepened within her as Lily listened to the distant bagpipe music Angus played with his heart. She listened to the noises of the night, the manor house creaks and groans, the hoots and chirps and howls of the nocturnal animals. She listened for familiar footsteps in the hall which never came.

The need for an arranged marriage no longer existed and 'twas plain Edan did not love her. She had no reason to linger. More determined than ever to depart in the morning, Lily would leave the Doonie Purse behind with the laird. She'd discovered the purse in Glen Carin and therefore 'twas rightfully his. The purse would enable him to restore Glen Carin and Cameron Castle in fine fettle. She had no use for gold.

Time passed slowly as she lay sleepless. The longcase clock chimed at every hour.

Lily had always found solace in her drawings, watching the birds spread their wings and fly. Enjoying the freedom from her mother she'd once wished for, the freedom she would envy when married to a man she did not love. But 'twas different now. Rather than fly away, she wished with all her heart to stay and nest. She loved the laird beyond what she ever thought possible.

But wishes were in vain. With Charlotte safely and happily wed and Edan with the means to succeed, Lily would do what she must and survive. She'd made up her mind to return to London and whatever fate Lady

Frances dealt her. After all, good, strong Scot blood ran through her veins.

There was only one thing left to do.

Opening her chamber door, Lily padded down the corridor to Edan's bedchamber. The floor stones felt frigid against her bare feet as she hurried down the hall. Halting in front of Edan's chamber, she regarded the latch as if it were alive and might bite her hand if she dared to touch. Something else played in her mind. If she opened his door and discovered Edan still awake, she would not turn and run. No. She would willingly fall into his bed.

Before she left Glen Carin behind, Lily yearned to feel the warmth of his hands exploring her body, the heat to rise within her, to hear his heart beating against hers. She had only the present. Tonight. To leave her legacy. She meant to make loving memories, memories enough to last her a lifetime. Memories to give her joy in the bleak world her mother had planned for her future. At that moment, Lily determined to follow her heart…and her heart had already passed before her into Edan's bedchamber.

She had no idea if he slept lightly, but in a matter of minutes she would know. Taking a deep breath, she filled her lungs with oxygen and courage before opening the door as quietly as possible. A thick tallow candle flickered in the dark, saving the chamber from complete pitch blackness. After closing the door behind her, Lily paused while her eyes adjusted to the darkness. The outline of a huge canopy bed in the center of the chamber came into focus. She could not distinguish the color of the damask drapes hung over a wall of windows. Edan's chamber was sparsely furnished with wash basin and a writing desk and chair dawn close to the fireplace. Only the snap and pop of the fire broke the silence—and her pounding heart. Her heart would give her away yet.

"Lilith? Is that ye?"

A strange combination of fear and surprise robbed her of speech.

"It must be," he said, answering his own question. "No one but ye would dare enter my chamber withoot a knock."

"I...I did not wish to wake you."

"Come closer."

She hummed. She hummed madly.

"Why do you hum?"

"I...I may have made a mistake in coming here." Flustered, Lily's hand trembled uncontrollably. She dropped the Doonie Purse.

"What was that?" Edan asked.

"A, a gift for you."

"Who brings a gift in the middle of the night?" He chuckled. "Ye have always been a bold lass. A minx with imagination. A bit of a bampot."

He'd called her crazy but with kindness and gentle chiding in his tone. She did not move, did not breathe.

"Ye do not need an excuse to enter my chamber, Lilith. Come closer."

Trembling from head to toe, she took one step closer.

He sat up slowly, blankets slipped away, revealing his bare chest.

Lily stood close enough to see the finely carved muscles of his chest, slashed with scars of battle and sprinkled with dark curls. A shiver ran through her.

Edan threw the covers back. Of course he slept unclothed. Her body warmed in places she'd never felt heat before.

When she closed her eyes, she heard his feet hit the floor. She opened her eyes to take in the man standing by his bed, taut and muscular from his calves to his torso to his biceps. Even with the scars of battle, his warrior body with muscles hewn strong and sinewy stirred a rush of desire within Lily like she had never known.

His voice was hushed, hardly audible above the crackling fire. "Ye have come to me."

"Before I go…"

He held out his hand. "Say no more about leaving. Let me love ye, lass."

She lowered her eyes, heart pounding furiously. After a lifetime of dreaming, she could make her dream a reality.

Lily slipped her hand in his and he drew her to him. He held her tightly against him. Through the thin fabric of her gown, she felt every hard plane of him. Heat spiraled through her like a thousand suns spreading through her veins.

Gently, with his thumb and forefinger, Edan raised her chin and brought his mouth down upon her upturned lips. She would never forget this kiss, nor this night with the man she knew now she'd loved all of her life. His tender kiss gave way to demand, delicious, and all-consuming.

Lily wrapped her arms around his neck and pressed herself to Edan as if she could melt into him. Becoming one in spirit and soul. Without releasing her mouth, he let out a low husky moan as he cupped first one breast and then the other. Her breasts swelled to fill his hand. Her entire body tingled with anticipation. The laird of her heart, muscular and virile, ignited a passion within Lily she'd never imagined existed. He set her free. Her heart danced with desire. Fierce desire. She purred softly as sweet honey moistness poured through her.

Edan pulled her down on his bed. Hungry with longing, she rolled and tumbled with him. She laughed with joy, cried with love. Each new sweet sensation took her breath away. Flesh to flesh. The compelling laird carried Lily to the highest star. She would never know a night like this again nor love like this again. She would find peace and happiness with her memory. Enfolded in the warmth of Edan's arms, Lily found never-ending promise.

The black pitch night gave way to a dusky gray dawn streaked with ribbons of plum and pink. Just before the gray sky gave way to dawn, Edan carried Lilith back to her chamber.

****

Of all the blasted pranks the reckless redhead had played on him when she was just a bairn, tonight she'd surpassed them all. He was done for. He'd never find the same, unbridled ecstasy with anyone else in his bed but the sleeping imp in his arms. Lilith Munro.

She gave a snuffle, a soft snoring sound. He carried her into her bedchamber and gently laid her down. "Good night, lass. Sleep ye well."

Back in his chamber, lying across his bed, Edan could not sleep. Wide awake and acutely alert, his nerves danced and sang. His heart pounded as visions of Lilith raced across his mind. Perfection. Tonight, she'd stood before him, bare and beautiful. She'd held her head high, her dark copper curls spilling past her shoulders. Edan had never seen such splendor in a woman. Never would he again. He knew. He knew then.

He loved Lilith. Perhaps he always had.

He did not own the black heart of his da, a man who could neither see beauty nor open his heart.

Edan rejoiced in Lilith's beauty.

Her body of porcelain and silk had beckoned to him and responded eagerly to his every touch. Driven by unrestrained passion, he'd made love to Lilith for hours. He'd brought her to happiness, to sighs of peace and completion…and the laughter of pure joy. While making love to the most vexing woman in his life, Edan found the most encompassing happiness he'd ever known.

No matter what mischief she'd played, past and present—as in wandering off and into the near arms of Brodie—he'd never thought of harming Lilith in any way. He'd never sought to punish her, even that day when she stolen his garments while he swam in the loch. No black-hearted man could withstand the light in her extraordinary eyes, the love in her heart.

Deep in contemplation, awareness he'd ignored for too long, Edan looked inward and finally recognized the man he'd become: laird, brother, warrior, farmer, and the man who had won Lilith's heart.

How could he spend another night without Lilith in his bed? How could he start another day without her by his side? How could he dream without her?

He bounded out of bed. "Bloody Hell!"

What was he to do with the fire inside? Pace until dawn? Box the night shadows? No. But what was he to do with these unfamiliar feelings that would not let him rest?

And then he remembered. Lilith had stolen into his chamber to bring a gift. Although at first Edan thought the gift was her, body and soul, he'd been wrong. She'd dropped the gift she'd brought. He'd heard the thump.

Lighting a fresh candle, Edan moved slowly about the room, shining the dim light on the floor, in the corners, nooks and crannies.

Just when he began to believe he'd imagined her excuse for coming to him, he found a dark object on the floor beside his washbasin. A brown leather pouch. Puzzled, he picked up the pouch, carrying the heavy purse to his bed. Could this be the Doonie Purse Lilith had spoken of?

Edan dinna believe in fairies. Still. He pulled at the drawstrings and turned the purse upside down. Out tumbled more gold than he'd ever seen. His heart leapt, racing with excitement. There was more than enough gold to restore both Glen Carin and Cameron Castle, purchase sheep, and plant barley. This gift of gold would make his dream of trading in his weapons for the trappings of a farmer come true.

Why hadn't Lilith kept the gold that would save her from Lady Frances's devious plans?

Because she believed in him.

Edan knew what he must do.

Chapter 12

The following morning Edan marched into the dining chamber. Resolved, decided, and determined.

Jamie, Angus and Finn regarded him in various stages of puzzlement.

"Station two men outside Lilith's bedchamber," he ordered Angus. "She is no' to leave. Tell her maid the plans have changed. The lady must sleep. She will no' be traveling today."

Frowning, Finn held his breakfast scone halfway to his mouth. "Yer holding the lass prisoner?"

"Nay. I am allowing Lilith time to come to her senses."

"Aye." Finn nodded as if he understood, but his expression said differently.

"Has Lilith lost her senses?" Jamie asked. "She appears fine to me."

"She planned to leave Glen Carin this morn in order to placate Lady Frances."

"In that case, Lilith is not fine. She may be deranged," the youngest Cameron declared. "If she should leave, Charlotte would be vera unhappy."

"I would be vera unhappy." Looking from one brother to the other, Edan made his intentions known. "Lilith is mine. She is meant to be mine. We will wed."

"Aye!" His brothers responded in unison, a chorus of hearty approval.

Having made his intentions known, Edan gave a curt nod of his head and stalked out of the room.

While Edan knew holding Lilith against her will would not set well with her, he did not know what else to do. He could not allow her leave. It had become abundantly clear to him—he could not live without her.

Plainly, she was meant to be his. If he hadn't actually known before she came to his bedchamber, he quickly came to the inevitable conclusion. No other woman had ever set him aflame in such a manner. No one else would do. It wasn't simply a case of want. He needed her. And his need was great. He needed her wisdom and her laughter. He needed to bury his face in the fiery mass of her silky hair and breathe in the sweet scent of roses. He needed to run his hands over the lush silkiness of her skin and feel her quiver beneath his fingers. Edan needed to love Lilith Munro for the rest of his life.

He returned to his chamber. He meant to spread the blankets and hide the evidence of Lilith's gift to him before Netta arrived to straighten his chamber. The gift of love.

He'd never felt about another woman the way he felt about Lilith. She had shown him the difference. He would do anything to make the tall, beautiful woman with the infectious laugh and shining eyes happy. The truth shocked him. But there it was. Edan loved Lilith. And he meant to tell her so.

Flinging open the drapes with more force than required, he gazed out over Cameron land. Ribbons of sun shone through the mist that hid the moors and the mountains. He smiled. He loved the Highlands with a passion only a Scotsman could know. And now he loved a woman with that same passion.

His body buzzed and hummed as it hadn't in years. He felt as if he could take on the entire French or British army. But he was a farmer now. Turning from the window, he moved toward the four-poster bed and tied back the ebony velvet drapes that gave warmth and privacy and offered lovers sanctuary. There was only one way he would let Lilith leave the Highlands now— over his dead body.

****

Lily awoke feeling achy but pleasantly content. A warmth and sense of well-being filled her. Last night she had been well loved. No matter what the future held, the memory of making love with Edan would last for the rest of her life. Oddly, though, she was back in her own bed, back in her chamber with no memory of how she had returned.

The growl of her stomach was the first signal that something was amiss. Lily bolted up in bed, wide awake. She tossed back her blankets, jumped from the bed, and threw open the drapes. The mist was lifting as it often did in late morning, but Jane hadn't woken her. In another hour it would be too late to set out for London. They would only be able to travel a few miles before nightfall. What had happened to Jane?

What had happened to Lily? What had happened to the Doonie Purse? She'd dropped it in Edan's bedchamber. But where? Had he found the treasure? Her pulse raced ahead of her heart. The last she remembered was curling against Edan's heat and falling asleep in his bed. He must have thought to salvage what he could of her reputation by returning her to her own bed in the dead of night.

Lily tugged on the bell pull and scrambled to dress in her traveling attire. Jane still hadn't arrived by the time Lily had brushed her hair and felt halfway decent in a highly unusual turn of events. Jane had always been loyal and devoted. She feared something untoward had happened to her young maid.

When she opened her door intending to investigate Jane's whereabouts, two strapping men stood guard on either side of the chamber door. Disconcerted, manners deserted her. "Who are you?" she asked. "And what are you doing here?"

One of the men responded gruffly without making eye contact. "Ye canna leave, milady,"

"I cannot leave my chamber?"

"Aye. 'Tis the laird's orders."

"I do not answer to the laird."

In concert, the men then stepped in front of Lily blocking her way. She had no doubt they would forcibly turn her back to her chamber if necessary. "I wish to see the laird immediately. Fetch Laird Cameron this minute."

With knit brows and dark frowns, the men looked at each other, clearly puzzled as to what to do, but neither moved.

Before she could repeat her demand, the clanging of the watch bell echoed through Glen Carin. Distant but urgent, the bell broke the impasse. The burliest of her guards shoved her back into the chamber. "We're here to protect ye. Get ye back in yer chamber."

"No! I do not require protection!" But as soon as the words were out, she knew her protest had fallen on deaf ears.

How could Edan hold her like a common prisoner

after they had made love through the night? He would hear about this. He could not keep her like a caged animal. Pressing her ear against the door, she heard one of the guards leaving, his footfalls racing down the corridor. Confident she had only one opponent, Lily decided to attempt to gain her release again. She pushed on the door. To no avail. The remaining guard, as big as a brick wall himself, evidently blocked the door.

Calling up every ounce of strength she possessed, Lily forced open one of the windows. Perhaps escape was possible. She stuck her head out and looked down. No, the drop caused her stomach to somersault.

"One coach!" The distant call of the Scot on watch alerted the residents of Glen Carin.

A coach? Someone, anyone, come to rescue her? Lily searched the tree lined, rocky road but could not yet see a coach. She ducked inside.

"Two coaches!"

Two?

Two coaches likely meant lost travelers in need of respite or directions. The slightest hope of leaving Glen Carin this day had just been crushed.

"Three coaches!"

Three coaches? Could it be royalty approaching Glen Carin? Who else traveled with three coaches?

She began pacing. Humming.

Soon she heard a shriek from the main hall. She pressed an ear against the door.

"What now?" Netta fairly screamed. "Who comes to Glen Carin now?"

Lily pounded on the door. "Let me out at once. At once! Do you hear?"

Netta could not hear Lily's cries, of course. And

the stubborn guard on duty at her door did not deign to reply.

She pounded again, pounding until her knuckles reddened as she vented her frustration. And then she heard a different voice outside her door.

"Is my sister confined to her chamber, sir?"

Charlotte? Of all people to come to Lily's rescue. Since they had been children, it had always been the other way around. Lily rescued Charlotte. She stifled an involuntary chuckle and stopped pounding on the door. "Charlotte, help me!"

"Release my sister at once."

Silence followed Charlotte's demand and the stomp of her foot.

"Well then," she huffed and let out a heavy sigh, "You leave me no choice."

Lily heard the man grunt. "Stand aside or I shall do it again."

She could only guess at what Charlotte had done, but not for a second did she believe the guard still stood. He sounded as if he were hopping. And whimpering.

"I believe you can come out now, Lily, but hurry before your guard regains his color."

Lily pushed hard, banging the door into her doubled- over guard. He fell to the floor.

"Why were you confined to your chamber?" Charlotte asked. "What did you do?"

"What did you do? To him," Lily pointed to the agonized guard.

Charlotte blushed, shrugged, and replied. "I jammed my knee in his private place."

Chuckling, Lily snatched her sister's hand and ran

down the corridor to the stairs.

Hearing the hubbub in the hall below as the coaches noisily pulled up to Glen Carin's main entrance, she came to an abrupt halt. Sensing the Camerons and their servants were gathered in the main hall, she took the moment to explain to Charlotte. "I am preparing to leave. There will be the devil to pay if I do not return to London quickly."

"But you came to be with Edan. I believed you and I would live here together as loving sisters, raising our babies together. You cannot leave."

Charlotte obviously possessed more of a romantic soul than Lily had ever guessed. Whenever had her sister blossomed into a daring young woman who would cause a grown man to fall to the floor in agony?

It made no matter. At the moment, Lily envied Charlotte for being able to envision her dream. "I would like that more than anything," she said to her sister, who showed just a bit of pouty lip. "But it is not to be. I must bargain with Mama. Be brave and let me leave. The demands of guests on the laird will help me slip away."

"Oh, dear." Charlotte's unhappy response was very nearly drowned out by the downstairs disturbance.

Edan's booming voice rang out. "Who comes, Finn?"

"Three coaches."

The laird's strides echoed in the corridor as he approached. "Open the door, Angus."

Lily tugged on her sister's hand. "Let us see who has arrived."

"Three coaches?" Charlotte said. "Perhaps it is the regent himself."

Lily did not answer as she and her wondering sister hurried down the steps to join Netta, Angus, Jamie, Finn, Maisie and two guards and a footman in the hall. A misfit welcoming committee to whoever had arrived if there ever was one, she thought.

Edan, who stood at the door, close to filling the space with his massive form, let out a deep rumble. "Oh, no."

'Twas a flat, sotto-voiced exclamation, unlike any Lily had ever heard from him before.

So much for Charlotte's hope the Prince Regent had arrived. But Lily could hardly contain her curiosity. Who was ascending the stairs even now out of sight? She strained to see.

"Lady Frances." Edan announced flatly.

Oh! No! Lily's first instinct was to flee to her bedchamber and ask one of her guards to protect her from her mama. But there was no time.

Edan bowed slightly. "Welcome back to Glen Carin, Lady—"

Lady Frances interrupted the laird in a piercing high pitch of annoyance. "Never you mind, Edan Cameron. I remember you as a trying young man plaguing my poor Lilith."

Lily had to credit Edan for his unwavering politeness. Her mama had yet to appear inside the hall. She could only surmise Lady Frances was taking the stairs slowly as befitted the queen she imagined herself to be.

Lily watched in mute horror as Lady Frances sailed into the hall, petite, imperious, and round as a cask of ale. The iron-queen was followed by a retinue of servants and luggage. Three coaches' worth. Her mother's amber cat-eyes flashed fury, her aged-yellowed ringlets dangling from the sides of her head bobbed with each step. But all eyes were on the bonnet of fantastical flowers which capped her top curls.

Lady Frances was clearly a fading beauty full of anger regarding the loss of her youth and fortunes. Deep brackets seemingly forced her tight lips downward as her gaze darted from person to person gathered to welcome her.

"Lady Frances." Edan bestowed a tight smile. "To what do we owe this visit?"

She glided straight up to him, burnishing a parasol. "My daughters! What have you done with my daughters, you wicked man?"

Lily rushed to her side. "The laird has done nothing, Mama. I meant to return home on this very day."

Lady Frances turned an icy gaze to Lily. "Yet you are here. Not at all where you told me you would be."

"Lily is not feeling well, dear Mama," Charlotte explained in a hurried defense of her sister.

At the moment, Lily's stomach tossed as if caught in a wild wind. Charlotte had never spoken truer words. She did not feel well at all. Her nerves threatened to undo her.

"And you?" Lily held her breath as Lady Frances spun on her youngest daughter. "You ran away with your sister. Did Lilith force you?"

"No, no."

"Did you believe such a childish action would prevent your nuptials? Oh, no, my dear. I would have sailed to the New World to bring you home."

Lily prepared to step in front of her sister to lend

protection as she'd done so many times, but Jamie quickly sprang to Charlotte's defense, stepping in front of her to shield his bride.

"Charlotte canna leave Glen Carin, for she is to wed me on the morrow."

"I. Beg. Your. Pardon?" Frost dripped from Lady Frances's lips. The matriarch gazed at Jamie through slitted eyes.

In the face of his future mother-in-law's displeasure, Jamie threw his shoulders back and straightened to a towering height. "'Tis a proud and happy man I am to claim Charlotte as my bride."

"You would marry a Scotsman?" Lily's incensed mother demanded through gritted teeth as she turned on Charlotte. "A man no better than a savage?"

"Mama, say no more!" Lily cried. "Jamie is a good man. Any woman would be happy to marry a Cameron."

Chin up in defiance, Charlotte stepped toward Lady Frances. "I will not marry any man but Jamie."

"You still have me," Lily reminded her mother. "I will return with you. I shall marry Viscount Whetfield."

"Och! No, you willna," Edan snapped, sending her a withering scowl. "Ye are betrothed, and I refuse to release ye."

Betrothed?

"Refuse to…to re…release me?" Lily stuttered, uncertain whether she should feel furious or exhilarated. *Betrothed?* Did he actually say betrothed? What lie was Edan telling?

"But I—"

Silencing Lily with a brief shake of his head and a warning glance, the most attractive laird in the land turned to her mother. Speaking coolly and quietly, Edan directed his full attention to the glaring little widow. "Lady Frances, ye are welcome to stay at Glen Carin until rested from your journey. But ye must return to London, happy in the knowledge yer daughters are safe in the Highlands, well-cared for, well-loved, and well-wed."

Had Edan actually said the words well-loved? Lily questioned what she thought she heard. He must have been speaking of Charlotte. Clearly, Jamie loved Charlotte very much.

Holding her breath, Lily waited for her mother's response to Edan's blunt dismissal. Her mind spun in a never-ending spiral of thoughts while Lady Frances grew crimson with rage.

"And tell me, Laird Cameron, with my daughters in the wilds of Scotland, how is an old woman like me supposed to support myself in the manner to which I have been accustomed?"

"I have the means. Ye will have my full support if you agree to leave Lilith and Charlotte here…where they belong."

Regarding him warily, her pale lips thinned. "Why should I believe you?"

"Because I am a man of honor. Ye shall have payment before leaving Glen Carin."

Lily's heart stopped. No! He meant to give Lady Frances support he could ill afford. He meant to give her the Doonie Purse in exchange for her freedom. "No! Laird Cameron—"

"Lilith!" Edan interrupted with a stern command, "Dinna meddle with a laird's business."

"But—"

Lady Frances cut her off, addressing Edan with the full force of her bitterness. "Do you expect me to believe you can support my Mayfair townhouse and servants as well as supply my entertainment allowance and my wardrobe requirements?"

"Aye."

"When you obviously cannot even afford new draperies?" She pointed to the threadbare drapes.

"Aye. I do, Lady Frances."

"No!" Lily cried.

Edan turned away from her mother. His deep indigo eyes softened as they gazed into Lily's. He spoke quietly so only she could hear. "You have humbled me, and I thank ye. You have given me a gift I value more greatly than the Doonie Purse. In time I will restore the land and Glen Carin. But I must have ye."

"Edan, you cannot hold me prisoner," she argued just as quietly, blinking back tears. "I shall return with my mother on the morrow."

The corner of his mouth hitched up in a smile both crooked and heart-stopping.

He took her breath away.

"Ye mistake my intentions."

Lily fell silent.

"Enough nonsense," Lady Frances declared, waving one gloved hand as if she were waving off an offensive odor. "I am a weary woman. What is this proposal?"

"No," Lily insisted beneath her breath, desperate to regain control of the situation. She quickly latched onto her mother's arm intent on dragging the woman away. "There is no proposal except what I propose. Mama, come with me."

"A moment!" Lady Frances's shrill cry caused goosebumps to rise on Lily's arms.

Charlotte seized Jamie's hand.

Angus started.

Finn's jaw dropped.

With nerves on edge, Lily watched in silence as her mother dug into the beaded reticule she carried and pulled out an envelope. Lady Frances held the battered envelope above her head, wielding the item as if it were a sword. "And this! Correspondence with a publishing house, Lilith, is beneath you," she raged. "'Tis for the common. What else have you done behind my back?"

By the looks of the envelope, it appeared her mother had not opened the unexpected correspondence. But then, Lily knew her difficult parent could barely read. As with so many other things in life, she relied on Lily and Charlotte. She could never be bothered with any sort of learning.

"Birds, Mama." She replied calmly, experiencing an unfamiliar sense of satisfaction. "I have been sketching birds."

Edan snatched the envelope from Lady Frances and handed it to Lily.

The correspondence was indeed from the publishing house. She thought it most likely a letter rejecting her illustrations and felt no need to tear the envelope open, surrounded as she was by trouble and sadness. At the moment, she felt totally unable to add to her own despair, the hollowness that had settled in her heart and deep in the pit of her stomach.

Edan turned from Lily to his housekeeper. "Netta, show Lady Frances to a bedchamber and see that her servants are comfortable."

"Jane will help you," Lily added quietly.

The sour-faced woman nodded to Lily, almost managing a smile. "Come ye," she said, gesturing with a sweep of her arm to Lady Frances and the waiting entourage,

Lady Frances bucked in shock at the servant's crude manner. She raised her head and narrowed her eyes. "Charlotte, I will deal with you later," she snipped. "Lily, you will come to my chamber in one hour," she bit out. "Do not be late."

"Yes, Mama." Lily often marveled how such a tiny woman could intimidate her, even now, it seemed. Ever since she could remember, Lily had done nothing but be obedient to her mother's rules and respect her forbidding parent. More than that, she'd attempted through the years to make her mother happy. But she'd never succeeded. Lady Frances held on to anger and envy like a dog with a bone. Instead of reaching for happiness from within, she found fodder in the outside world to add more poison to her soul daily.

There was no help for her Mama. A truth that saddened Lily.

Her mother shot one last withering glance toward Edan and sailed from the room led by Netta and followed by her entourage of servants.

Edan placed a warm, consoling hand on her shoulder. "Lilith, I would have a word with ye before yer private talk with Lady Frances."

She nodded, knowing nothing he could say or do would change her mother's mind—or hers. There seemed no use in arguing at this point.

Tight-lipped Edan strode from the room followed by Finn, Angus and Jamie.

Charlotte hurried to Lily's side. "Do not return with Mama. You are happy here. There is a lovely gleam in your eyes and lightness in your step. You belong at Glen Carin. You belong with the laird, with Edan. And with me," she added with a wistful smile. "Just as I told you, the laird has the means to send Mama away with the support she requires."

"No, it cannot be. Not at the expense of Glen Carin and all who reside here."

"Did you not hear Edan? He has a proposal to take care of Mama. Besides, even if he changes his mind, Mama will find a way. She always has. I know it sounds cruel, but our mother has never worried about us. She would have me marry a man who is thought to have killed his wife—and now she will have you do the same. 'Tis time for Mama to save herself."

Lily gave her beautiful sister a hug. Amazing how in just a short matter of time her sibling had become as wise as she was beautiful. "Perhaps we can arrange a marriage for her?"

Charlotte's eyes twinkled. "We can do no worse in finding a husband for her than Mama has done for herself in the past."

"I will think on it, Charlotte."

"Would you like me to help you? I can think of many reasons why you belong at Glen Carin and why Mama should leave without us."

"You've given me enough to ponder, thank you."

Lily could not easily shake the compassion she still felt for her mama. The tiny tyrant was her mother after all. Lady Frances had spent a lifetime wallowing in unhappiness and blaming other people for her discontent.

Releasing her sister with a light kiss on her cheek, Lily fled to her chamber. Tossing the correspondence from the publishing house on the bed, she followed, flinging herself on the four-poster forlornly. More than anything, Lily longed to remain at her home in Glen Carin. She belonged here in the Highlands. Her heart and soul had told her so long ago. The truth had been whispered on the wind. Last night encompassed in Edan's arms, her feelings were confirmed. She would never love another man.

With the contents of the Doonie Purse, Edan could restore the clan lands, purchase Brodie's land and take care of the Cameron brothers and their wives in comfort, including Charlotte. The laird could not refuse her gift. The purse belonged in Glen Carin for Glen Carin, and Lily meant to make certain her da's wishes were respected.

No matter how horrid Lady Frances could be, she was vulnerable. Without Lily's help, she would manage poorly. Her very presence in Glen Carin testified to the fact. Otherwise, the disagreeable woman would not have made the journey to the Highlands she loathed. Lily's choice was clear. She would return with her mother and marry Whetfield or whomever could support Lady Frances in the manner she'd become accustomed.

Despair curled through Lily like thick, dark smoke, smothering her ability to breathe. Knowing she could not feel worse that she did, she reached for the envelope from Grammarcy Publishing House.

Chapter 13

Steeling herself, Lily knocked on her mother's bedchamber at the appointed time. Lady Frances's maid Eloise quickly opened the door and stood back waiting for Lily to enter the darkened, musty guest chamber. The drapes were drawn, and a fire blazed in the fireplace. If she were in the least unnerved by small, enclosed places smelling of smoke, tallow, and moldering ruin, Lily would have run from her mother's chamber in hysterics. Not a breath of air moved. She feared she and her mother might quickly suffocate in the closed space.

One strategically placed lantern and several candles flickered throughout the bedchamber giving it an eerie glow.

Squinting, Lily slowly stepped into her mother's quarters. "Mama?"

"Here." Lady Frances's weak reply came from the corner bed. "The barbarian has forced me to take to my bed. 'Tis evil to place me in this worn bedchamber. The laird means to kill me."

Lily hurried to the bedside. "Barbarian? Kill you? Mama, you exaggerate."

Her mother, propped up by a number of pillows in the elaborately carved four-poster bed, held a cloth to her head. "Edan Cameron, the laird of this horrid cold and damp manor is a barbarian. Did you not hear how he spoke to me?"

"Mama—"

"He addressed me with contempt rather than the respect to which I am owed."

Lily swiftly changed the subject. "You wanted to see me?"

"Why did you come to Glen Carin, forcing me to chase after you? Why did you bring your sister to this dreadful country? Have you no shame?"

"I came...to refresh my memories."

"Clearly, you have lost your mind. You are as reckless as your father before you," she bit out. "I thought you my intelligent child."

Lily sucked in a surprised breath. For the first time in her memory Lady Frances had come close to paying her a compliment. "You have *two* intelligent daughters, Mama. And this is my father's country, his home," she said softly and calmly. It would go easier for Charlotte and her if she could make her mother understand. "Strong Scot blood runs through my veins."

"Unfortunate," Lady Frances snapped. "Prepare to leave as soon as I am well. Glen Carin unnerves me. Always did." She sniffed as if something lay dead behind the walls. Her snappish tone shifted into a whine. "I've had to take laudanum."

"You will soon sleep then," Lily assured her.

"No. I shall require another dose just to close my eyes."

"Perhaps we should talk later."

"No, we will talk now," her mother insisted with a yawn.

Lily began to back away. "You've made an arduous journey."

Her mother's cat eyes flicked open, locking on Lily's. "You gave me no choice by running off. Thank goodness I arrived in time. Charlotte is to be married in days to Jamie Cameron? A most improper notion!"

"Improper?"

"I have planned a proper, elegant wedding fit for a princess. She will be wed in Westminster Cathedral with hundreds of flower bouquets and the finest of the ton in attendance."

"Mama, Charlotte does not wish a wedding spectacle. A wedding extravaganza is your desire."

"She will do as I say."

"Charlotte is betrothed to Jamie."

Lady Frances tossed the cloth she'd been holding to her head at Lily. "I shall not allow my beautiful daughter to marry a savage when a titled man of means awaits her."

"Mama—"

"Do not dare to be impertinent with me," she warned.

"Never," Lily murmured.

Lady Frances let out a moan only the finest actresses might duplicate. "You lied to me, saying you were off to the Duchess Mary of Fairlyham's funeral in Bath. What have I done to deserve lies from my children?"

"We did attend the funeral…before we continued our journey to Glen Carin. If I'd told you the truth, you would have stopped us."

"For your own good." Inhaling deeply, she released another, weaker moan. "I don't know how you have stood to linger in the Highlands, especially in Glen Carin all this time."

"Mama, we have only been in the Highlands a little more than two weeks."

"Much too long. The Cameron men are not worth your time."

Lily tapped her foot, growing more impatient with her mother by the moment. "No, Mama. Laird Cameron and his brothers are good men."

"How can you say that when Jamie Cameron has hypnotized your sister into believing she is in love with him? A Scot!"

"He did not kidnap her nor hypnotize her. Jamie loves Charlotte and she chose to come with me to Glen Carin of her own accord. Charlotte chose to be with Jamie."

"She has lost her mind. I shall talk sense into her. She cannot survive life here."

"Charlotte has survived very well. Mama, please leave her be," she pleaded. "Can you not see how happy she is?"

"Your sister is too young to know if she is happy or not."

"She deserves to be happy." *And I do too.*

"Without Viscount Whetfield's purse, how will I survive?"

In danger of losing her composure, Lily turned on her heel, intent on making her retreat from the cloying room and her mother's malicious mind as quickly as possible.

"Wait!"

"What?" She'd almost made it out the door. Her hand stayed on the door latch.

"Has the laird had his way with you?"

Mother Have Mercy!

Lily whirled around to face Lady Frances. "Believe me or not, but Edan is neither a barbarian nor a savage. He is most extraordinary, a good and honorable human being." *And I will not ever share the most incredible night of my life with you.*

Lady Frances scowled. "We shall return to London on the day after tomorrow. I shall be rested by then."

"I cannot ask Charlotte—"

Closing her eyes, Lady Frances sank back against the pillows, waving Lily off in a pitiful voice, "Lilith. Go. You have made my aching head worse. Prepare to leave for London."

Lily dropped her hand from the door and turned to confront her mother. "No, Mama, I am not returning with you."

"Of course you will return with me."

"No." She dug in her pocket for the letter she'd thrust there minutes before. Lily held up the correspondence from Grammarcy Publishing in triumph. Much to her surprise, the letter held the means to support her demanding mother until such time as Lady Frances married again. Lily had no doubts that her mother would marry again, sooner rather than later. "My book of bird illustrations has been purchased, and the publishing company has asked for another."

Lady Frances bolted upright from her mountain of pillows. "Bird pictures?"

"My illustrations have earned the means to allow you to live for a time as you are accustomed—if you spend wisely."

"If? If I spend…" her voice trailed off into shocked silence.

"Wisely, Mama."

"Are you offering me an allowance? From bird pictures? My own daughter!"

"Aye. In return I am asking you to leave Charlotte at Glen Carin. And me as well."

"You are no child of mine!" Lady Frances shrieked.

Lily thought her mother was most likely right. She was her father's daughter. "'Tis your choice, Mama. I have made mine."

Her enraged mother threw the goblet from her bedside table at Lily. "You will rue this day!"

With a quick sidestep, Lily ducked, and the goblet shattered against the wall. She stared at the annihilation in surprise. Lady Frances possessed a far better aim than she'd guessed.

Drawing herself up to her full, proud height, Lily opened the door. "Goodnight, Mama."

"Ungrateful chit!"

Lily gently closed the door behind her, leaned against it, and closed her eyes. A heavy sadness for the woman who bore her weighed in Lily's heart. But in mere moments, Lily floated on the airy wings of relief. A great weight had been lifted. She would no longer bear witness to her mother's tantrums or be the object of her rage. At last Lily was free to be her own woman.

Not for the first time she wondered how Lady Frances could possibly be her mother.

****

Feeling the need to regain her composure, Lily headed for the stables, thinking to ride with the wind. 'Twas an excellent way to restore inner calm.

Dragon whinnied when she entered the stables and for an unguarded moment she thought to have the stable boy saddle Edan's horse for her. Instead, she told Malcom, "I should like to ride Bonnie."

"Aye, milady."

As she set out from the stables, the chill of the gray day seeped through her bones and settled in the moors. The haunting beauty of the Highlands surrounded her and caused her heart to sing with joy.

Lily hadn't gone far when she heard the sound of thunderous hooves.

Edan chased after her, racing astride his gelding. She reined in her sweet mare to properly greet him, a powerful striking figure of a man, all brain and brawn. "I have welcome news for you," she told him. "My mother is far too exhausted to attend supper this evening."

He hiked a dark brow. "Aye? I went to see Lady Frances, but when I heard her wailing, I turned about. I shall save my speech for another day."

"'Tis what Mama does when disappointed. She shouts and shrieks."

"Was she disappointed to discover Charlotte will marry Jamie?"

"Yes, you might say that. Mama rues the day she decided on this journey to Glen Carin."

Pressing his lips together, he nodded. "Nonetheless, I shall visit Lady Frances this eve."

She shook her head. "'Tis not a good time."

"Och! And what would be a good time with yer mother?"

"Tomorrow, perhaps. I have given Lady Frances good news. My book of bird illustrations has been sold and another has been requested. The proceeds will support my mother in fine fashion for a time. Until she remarries."

He turned to her, wearing a puzzled frown. "Ye have sold sketches of birds?"

Laughing, she replied in the native language which had become second nature. "Aye."

"Ye must be a vera excellent artist."

"I am," she replied proudly.

"And ye alone can support Lady Frances until she finds a new husband?"

Lily nodded emphatically. "Indeed. And I have just the man in mind."

"Whetfield?"

She smiled. "If Mama chooses."

"Yer too clever, and too generous, Lilith." Dismounting, he gestured for her to do the same.

Lightheaded with happiness, she slid into Edan's waiting arms. "Nay. I have what I've long wished. I've gained my freedom and may live my life as I choose. As free as a bird."

"Ye are no bird," he said, holding her by the shoulders. "Ye are the lass I wish to marry."

Her heart skipped. Her cheeks warmed. She lowered her gaze. "We have not discussed terms of an arranged marriage and—"

"Ye have given me a gift I have not earned. It belongs to ye."

"You speak of the Doonie Purse. 'Tis real, as you know now, and filled with gold. My da would have wanted you to restore Glen Carin using the contents. He left the purse in Glen Carin, in the Longcase clock for a reason. I discovered the purse but understand he meant to provide for his beloved home."

"Aye, and his beloved daughters?"

Shrugging, Lily twirled from his hold and strolled toward the nearest pine. Her little mare followed. "With the contents of the Doonie Purse and the profits Jamie brought from the last sale, you shall have the funds to purchase the Brodie land, a herd of astonishing Black Faced Sheep and whatever your heart desires."

He took both of her hands in his. "My heart desires you. Lilith. Will ye be my wife?"

"Please do not feel you must marry me simply because—"

"I love ye." His blue-gray gaze locked on hers.

She could not speak for a moment, could not believe what she'd heard. "Eh?"

"I love ye, Lilith," he grinned. "Even though ye be the bane of my boyhood."

Laughter bubbled up from her toes. At once she felt as giddy as if she'd sipped one too many drams of ale. "Say again, a wee bit louder, if you please."

"I love ye, Lilith Munro," he roared, loudly enough for everyone within a mile of where they stood to hear. His rich voice, his deep belly laugh of pure happiness echoed through the gathering dusk and beyond. "I love ye!"

Lily launched herself into his arms. "I have been waiting my entire life to hear you say those words."

"Lass, ye'll be hearing those words forever, for the rest of yer life." Edan enfolded her in his arms.

Lily feared she might swoon. If it were not for Dragon plodding up behind her, she might have fallen. Being able to rest against Edan's huge gelding saved her from further mortification.

"Ye have not given me an answer," the impatient laird prompted. "Will ye marry me?"

"Aye," she laughed. "Aye, I will marry you."

Gathering her into his arms, the great Laird Edan Cameron kissed Lily deeply, thoroughly. When at last he released her, Lily swayed like a willow in a windstorm.

Thrusting his arm out to the empty moor before him, he made an unexpected declaration, "I shall build a cottage here where we can escape when Glen Carin becomes too crowded with Charlotte and Jamie."

"Brilliant!"

"We shall steal away to make love through the night," he said, looking out over the moor.

Edan was lost to Lily for the moment, she knew, deeply rooted in his imagination, envisioning each room of their love cottage. He took no notice when she hitched up her skirts and jumped aboard his horse—no easy task.

He noticed when Dragon sprinted forward. "Lilith!"

Damn the minx!

"Shameless ye are! Lilith!"

Her laughter carried on the wind…and mingled with his.

A word about the author…

Sandra Madden is a former writer/producer for a Miami PBS television station where she specialized in women's issues and public affairs programming. Before turning to writing full time, Sandra also held positions as a radio copy and promotion writer in both Miami and Los Angeles.

Ms. Madden is the published author of fifteen historical and contemporary romance novels, translated and issued in over six languages. She also co-authored the memoir of her late husband Dave Madden, most well-known for his role as Reuben Kincaid on *The Partridge Family*. *Reuben Kincaid Remembered* is the former comedian and television actor's story from humble beginnings to worldwide fame.

Sandra is a member of NINC and the Florida Writers Association.

Find her at:

www.sandramadden.com

Thank you for purchasing
this publication of The Wild Rose Press, Inc.

For questions or more information
contact us at
info@thewildrosepress.com.

The Wild Rose Press, Inc.
www.thewildrosepress.com

A word about the author...

A voracious reader her whole life, author Susan Payne loved the written word. When reading more than fifty books per month wasn't enough, she decided to allow her mind to take flight and write all the many stories that kept intruding into her life. She blended her love of history and her love of words to create over eighty stories. All historical and centering on a couple finding love and a happy ever after together.

You may contact Susan at:
http://www.authorsusanpayne.com or
authorspayne@gmail.com

Thank you for purchasing
this publication of The Wild Rose Press, Inc.

For questions or more information
contact us at
info@thewildrosepress.com.

The Wild Rose Press, Inc.
www.thewildrosepress.com